The Key of Knowledge

Keys of Lazarus

Michael Lackey

Published by Seven Crows Publications, 2018.

This is a work of fiction. Similarities to real people, places, or events are entirely coincidental.

THE KEY OF KNOWLEDGE

First edition. February 23, 2018.

Copyright © 2018 Michael Lackey.

Written by Michael Lackey.

To all the lost souls seeking knowledge...

It is within you.

Prologue

John 11 King James Version (KJV)

1 Now a certain man was sick, named Lazarus, of Bethany, the town of Mary and her sister Martha.

2 (It was that Mary which anointed the Lord with ointment, and wiped his feet with her hair, whose brother Lazarus was sick.)

3 Therefore his sisters sent unto him, saying, Lord, behold, he whom thou lovest is sick.

4 When Jesus heard that, he said, this sickness is not unto death, but for the glory of God, that the Son of God might be glorified thereby.

5 Now Jesus loved Martha, and her sister, and Lazarus.

6 When he had heard therefore that he was sick, he abode two days still in the same place where he was.

7 Then after that saith he to his disciples, let us go into Judaea again.

8 His disciples say unto him, Master, the Jews of late sought to stone thee; and goest thou thither again?

9 Jesus answered, Are there not twelve hours in the day? If any man walk in the day, he stumbleth not, because he seeth the light of this world.

10 But if a man walk in the night, he stumbleth, because there is no light in him.

11 These things said he: and after that he saith unto them, Our friend Lazarus sleepeth; but I go, that I may awake him out of sleep.

12 Then said his disciples, Lord, if he sleep, he shall do well.

13 Howbeit Jesus spake of his death: but they thought that he had spoken of taking of rest in sleep.

14 Then said Jesus unto them plainly, Lazarus is dead.

15 And I am glad for your sakes that I was not there, to the intent ye may believe; nevertheless let us go unto him.

16 Then said Thomas, which is called Didymus, unto his fellow disciples, let us also go, that we may die with him.

17 Then when Jesus came, he found that he had lain in the grave four days already.

18 Now Bethany was nigh unto Jerusalem, about fifteen furlongs off:

19 And many of the Jews came to Martha and Mary, to comfort them concerning their brother.

20 Then Martha, as soon as she heard that Jesus was coming, went and met him: but Mary sat still in the house.

21 Then said Martha unto Jesus, Lord, if thou hadst been here, my brother had not died.

22 But I know, that even now, whatsoever thou wilt ask of God, God will give it thee.

23 Jesus saith unto her, Thy brother shall rise again.

24 Martha saith unto him, I know that he shall rise again in the resurrection at the last day.

25 Jesus said unto her, I am the resurrection, and the life: he that believeth in me, though he were dead, yet shall he live:

26 And whosoever liveth and believeth in me shall never die. Believest thou this?

27 She saith unto him, Yea, Lord: I believe that thou art the Christ, the Son of God, which should come into the world.

28 And when she had so said, she went her way, and called Mary her sister secretly, saying, The Master is come, and calleth for thee.

29 As soon as she heard that, she arose quickly, and came unto him.

1 Lucy

It was raining again. Drop after drop splashed against the dark mahogany box. People were shielding their heads with papers, while others had no option but to scurry off. Her face was already wet with tears, but Lucy didn't notice the rain, or the people for that matter. Her red eyes were fixed on the flower arrangement being pelted by the falling drops. She sensed a tug on her sleeve and could make out a voice behind her urging her to step away to allow the Grave Bots to do their work. She remained, staying to watch as the center of her world was lowered six feet into the ground. The large gray stone at the head of the unforgiving hole read, 'A man of many talents. Loving husband, father, and grandfather. Conrad Otto 1973-2058.' Today Lucy buried her grandfather - the only person she had left in her life.

With tears streaming down her face she whispered desperately, "What am I supposed to do now? I can't be alone, Gramps. We always took care of each other..." her gaze fixed on the tombstone as if it might answer. Cold and silent it offered no reply.

"You always told me I didn't need you, that it was you who needed me. Well, Gramps? Who will need me now?"

She knelt to brush away the mud that the Grave Bots had splashed onto the head marker. "No, this is wrong. Stupid bots can't do anything right!" Even as she cleared the stone, the rain splashed more mud around the bottom. As she continued to clear away the dirt, her eyes were drawn to a strange marking on the bottom of the tombstone. It was a symbol she'd never seen: two intertwined letters - S & R.

What is this? Why is it here? Lucy began to think they must have messed up his stone! With sharp anger dripping from each word like the rain falling from the tips of her blue hair Lucy proclaimed, "They trash bins on either side of her. She concentrated on deep breaths, in through her nose and out through her mouth. Her eyes remained closed as she struggled to keep her head from spinning. Something bumped against her shoe and she looked down to see a shiny brass ball lying in front of her. It started to vibrate and buzz. When it stopped, a bell rang, and another white envelope popped out from a slot on the top of the ball.

"Really? This again? Come on!" she said snatching up the envelope. The little round bot let out a puff of steam and played a cheerful tune before rolling away. Lucy tore open the envelope and found yet another piece of the faded yellow paper. "What else could it be?" she said aloud in a disdainful tone, and then thought to herself. "I'm starting to think someone is playing with me." The anger rose in her belly and erupted from her throat as she screamed "I'M NOT IN THE MOOD FOR GAMES!" After a 10-second meditative breathing session, she looked down at the paper, which read, '**Come to.**' "Well, let's add it to my collection," she said shrugging. Lucy folded the paper and shoved it into her pocket along with the other pieces. Sitting down on a pile of boxes, she ran her hands through her brightly colored hair. "Am I going insane?" she wondered aloud, "No, surely I'm cursed. That's it, cursed or something. Why else would I lose the only person in the world that cared about me, then have the most powerful woman in the world want me dead? All for something I haven't a clue about! I don't understand..."

A woman's soft voice filled her ears, "Then maybe you should be educated in the things you don't understand."

Lucy jumped forward, stumbling over a couple of bags of old cans and day-old sprouts. Looking up, she held her hands in front of her face to try to shield herself. "Please, don't hurt me!" After a moment of not being hit, mauled, or sliced to bits, Lucy moved her hands and saw the woman standing over her.

"Why on Earth would I hurt the granddaughter of the one and only Conrad Otto?" the woman asked, extending a hand to help Lucy up.

"It's you! The one from the graveyard!" Lucy said in shock. "How did you know my grandfather? Today has been extremely hectic, and eventful in ways I'd like to forget. I would appreciate a straight answer from someone, for once."

The woman looked around. "Here is not the place, and now is not the time. You will know where to go soon enough. I will be in touch, Miss Lucy Ducit." With that, she turned and started walking straight for the dead end of the alley. She pulled a brass disc from her old brown side purse as she walked. Lucy was watching in utter confusion as the woman turned to face her and dropped the round, metal sheet onto the ground. A series of beeps rang out, and it grew to the size of a garbage can lid. The woman smiled, and then she stepped onto it. Suddenly, eight tiny cylinders sprang from the surrounding edges. Steam rushed from each cylinder as the woman began to lift off the ground.

Lucy ran toward her. "Can I at least get your name? Please... I just need some truth to hold onto in this chaos," she pleaded.

The elderly woman flashed another smile and said, "Stan. My name is Stan."

Lucy watched as Stan flew up and out of sight. On the bottom of the flying disc, something familiar caught her eye. "That same symbol! What does S & R stand for? Is Stan the one that put that on Gramp's marker?" she thought to herself.

She felt confident that answers would be coming, and Stan would help her. At least, she hoped Stan would help her.

letter like a magnet and mended the tear. "This is just... just impossible. Whoever made this is a genius!"

She picked the paper back up. "What does this symbol mean?" she thought. "Surely Stan's not working for the Countess... No. If she was, whatever I've gotten myself into, she would have arrested me already or I'd be dead."

Lucy jumped to her feet as a loud knock boomed from her front door. Quietly, she slid with her back to the wall, making her way to the peephole.

"A courier? A human courier? For me? Human couriers are only for the wealthy and the important,"

she whispered.

Lucy slowly cracked the door open making sure the chains were still locked and in place. "I'm sorry, there must be some mistake. You must have the wrong address."

She had started to close the door when the courier said, "Lucy Ducit? The paperwork says you would try to refuse, but this is your name. Am I correct? We're not in the habit of making mistakes here at UPS (United Personal Services). You have to accept this parcel, or I don't get paid."

Lucy peeked through the crack of the door, under the chains. "Show me the package." The courier sighed heavily and held the package up to show her. "That's Gramp's handwriting," Lucy said in shock. She slid the chains from their locks and opened the door just enough for the package to fit through.

The young man held up a clipboard with an ID scan attached. "Just hold the pen sensor and smile at the pretty purple light." The pen flashed a fluorescent light, and the currier snidely said, "Now, was that so hard?" She handed the pen sensor back through the crack but just as he almost had a hold of it, she dropped it to the floor and slammed the door shut, locking it just as quickly.

"They don't pay me enough for this! That's why we shouldn't come to this part of town," he mumbled as he walked away.

She walked back to the table and carefully opened the sides to avoid tearing the writing on the front. "What is this?" she gasped as she lifted a box from the packaging. "This is gorgeous! I have never seen craftsmanship this detailed before," she thought to herself. She examined every side of the box that lay before her. "This is extraordinary, Gramps had to have paid an engineer a lot of money for this." The box she held in her hands was extremely intricate. Light and dark brass gears fit together as if they were formed *from* the box, not attached *to* it. No bigger than a shoe box, but much heavier. The brass looked worn, but intentionally made that way. She saw scratches on the side that resembled knife marks. "Did someone try to open this?" she thought as she felt the indentations.

"I don't see a latch on this thing," she mused aloud. Trying to be careful, she turned the box over in her hands looking for a keyhole, buckle, or some way to open it. "I must be missing something. Think, Lucy, think." Lucy sat the box on the table and looked harder at the scratches hoping to see an opening. "Another dead end," she huffed. "How do you open a lock that doesn't have a key?" She stared at the mysterious box, concentrating on the gears to one side. She soon noticed that they connected to several smaller gears, which, in turn, all led to a dial in each of the four corners. Each one consisted of numbers ranging from zero to nine.

"What numbers would Gramps use to lock away something important?" she mumbled behind her hands that were rubbing her face. "There's his birthday..." she thought. Turning the knobs to 1973 and holding her breath, nothing happened. "Mom's birthday!" She twisted the knobs again, and still nothing happened. "What about..." then it hit her. "Something important, of course!" she squealed. She turned the dial on the top left corner to the number two. Moving over to the top right corner, she stopped at zero. Next was the bottom left corner, this one she spun to the number three. The last one, the bottom right, Lucy turned the knob stopping on the number nine. "There, 2039 the year I was born."

All the gears dropped and locked into place. Slowly they turned, tooth in groove, round and round, exposing the center as a key popped up. Lucy turned the key to the left and heard pistons releasing pressure, unlocking all around the edges. She opened the box to find a simple, brown leather book. No markings or lettering. Just an old, worn journal with a single frayed leather strap wrapped around it. Lucy picked the book up and untied the strap.

Opening the front cover, she saw handwritten text that read, "*This is the secret and private journal of Conrad Otto, Synod of Reaping. Date: 12 October 1994. Today my eyes were opened to my destiny.*" The next page had the same intertwined S & R symbol she had seen on his tombstone and the flying disc. "Synod of Reaping? Reaper! That's what that jerk, Martin, called me!" She hastened to close the diary and stood back from the table. She wrung her hands together as sweat started to bead on her forehead. She was having trouble catching her breath, and her heart raced. "What were you a part of, Gramps?" she said as the yellow piece of paper caught her eyes again. "Fifth Avenue and East Eighty-Second. I need to find Stan."

Lucy took the piece of paper and her grandfather's diary and put them into her backpack. Running out the door, leaving everything behind, Lucy headed for the heart of the slums of New York... Fifth Avenue.

Out on the street, Lucy hailed a steamer cab. The large, bright yellow cab pulled up in front of her. Steam rushed out of the exhaust as the husky driver rolled down the window and asked, "Ver to?"

"Fifth Avenue and East Eighty-Second, please," Lucy replied.

"Nyet. Zat's no place for leetle girl. You pick better place," he demanded in a thick accent.

Lucy dug into her front pocket and pulled out some cash. "No, I need to go to Fifth and East Eighty-Second."

The driver expelled a huff of hot air out through his thick, burly mustache, mumbling words Lucy was sure she didn't want to know. Gears turned, weights moved from side to side, and the door dropped like a drawbridge. As Lucy settled into the backseat, she could see the driver's picture ID and name displayed on the dash. "So, your name is Jemison?" she asked trying to make conversation.

"Yah, Jemison Alexeev. You surrre you vant go to Fifth Avenue? Not much zerre," he replied.

"Yes, I'm meeting someone there, so I'll be all right..." she said confidently, to which she added "I hope," under her breath.

It didn't take as long as Lucy had thought to arrive at Fifth Avenue. There was never much traffic anymore on this end. The steamer cab pulled up in front of a huge building with three large archway windows. The middle one had what looked to be doors boarded up. The architecture was charming and had large steps leading up to huge columns. The building was a modern-day castle styled from forgotten days. Even now, as it sat there covered in graffiti and with trash blowing everywhere, it still commanded respect. Lucy handed Jemison his money before she exited the cab.

"You vant I should stay?" he asked trying to convince her.

"No, thank you. I'll be fine. Thanks for the concern though," Lucy replied as she hopped out of the cab. Jemison leaned out of his window and handed her a card with his information on it.

"You ever need rride back, you kall Jemison."

Lucy smiled and nodded her head as the cab rolled away, blowing steam out from its upper pipes. When it had gone, she took the piece of faded yellow paper from her backpack and looked again at the information.

"This is the right place. I don't understand. There's nothing here," she said, looking around for any signs of Stan.

"Oh, but I'm here." The man's voice startled her. "And I see you're here. Tell me, are you lost? That would make it so much better if you were lost, sweet cakes."

Lucy started to back away. "I don't have any money, I swear! Please, leave me alone," she said, her voice shaking with fear.

"It's not your money I want, honey. What I want is..."

A loud snap filled the air forcing the man to his knees. As he grasped at a leather strap around his throat, Stan stepped out of the shadows holding the handle of a bullwhip. Coming closer to the stricken man, she said, "The lady asked you to leave her alone. I believe she even said please. I suggest you listen." Pulling on the whip, Stan released the man's neck. As she did so, he leapt forward trying to rush the older woman. "You just don't listen, do you, deary?" Stan had grabbed a small brass barreled pistol from the holster strapped to her thigh, and just as the man made a vain attempt to stop in his tracks, he felt the cold metal pressing against his forehead. "Now the way I see it, I can pull this trigger, making a mess of you and myself; or, pay attention to this part now, son, you can remove your shoes and pants and start running in that direction there," she threatened, while pointing to the right. Sweat started to bead across his forehead, swirling around the indentation formed by the end of the barrel. Shaking from head to toe, he shifted his eyes to Lucy.

She crossed her arms. "You're seriously looking to me for help?"

The man closed his eyes and took a deep breath. He slowly kicked off his boots and tossed them to the side. "My pants, too? Really?" he asked, almost in tears.

"You could have just walked away, but you went and made me pull old trusty here. That deserves a little more," Stan told him.

The air expelling from his rib cage wasn't the only sign of nervousness. His hands shaking, he could barely unbuckle his belt. He glanced up at Stan hoping for a change of heart. "That's a nice belt! Leather?" she asked. "Toss that over here, then drop the trousers and run. We don't want to see your pasty butt any longer than we have to," Stan told him as she pressed a little harder with the pistol.

Dropping his pants to the ground, he stepped out of them and stood there frozen in fear.

"Gross!" Lucy started to dry heave.

"Now run!" Stan shouted and fired a single shot directly above his head.

"Did you see that? I think he soiled himself!" Stan laughed as the man ran. "We better get inside before we catch a whiff of that," she added, still laughing as she pinched her nose.

"Where did you learn to do that?" Lucy asked her.

"All in due time, dear. Now come on, we don't want to cause any more of a commotion," Stan told her as she led her toward the building. They walked up the steps to where the doors were once opened to anyone. Now they stood barred shut, and covered in spray paint.

"How do we get in?" Lucy asked.

Stan smiled, "Oh, you have a lot to learn, kiddo."

She turned toward the graffiti on the boards. In particular, a section in bright colors that read, "Rangers takE All Prisoners!" She used her index finger to trace the letters R.E.A.P that Lucy had noticed were all capitalized. The floor shook briefly and then started to lower them deep beneath the building. "It's okay, Lucy. You'll see."

Lucy looked around in amazement. Gears the size of buildings were being turned by smaller gears and wires. All turning, whirring and whining to keep up.

"Your grandfather did most of this," Stan told her. "He was certainly a man of many talents."

"I'm beginning to think Gramps was more than just a nice old man," Lucy said, unable to hide her awe-struck expression.

Stan laughed out loud. "You have no idea, kiddo." She placed her arm around her shoulders. "You have no idea..."

4 Synod of Reaping

The platform touched down, and they appeared to be inside what appeared to be the world's largest workshop. Every kind of tool, spanner, shaper, or machine one could imagine, and a few Lucy was sure didn't have names, were there. Tables were piled high with gears, and free-standing walls were covered with blueprints tacked to them. A tall automated brass and gas walkabout bot approached them. "Welcome back, Ms. Stanley. I see you brought a guest."

"Indeed, Walter. This is Lucy Ducit..."

"Lucy! My, you have grown." Walter interrupted as Stan shot the bot a glare. Walter stopped, stuttered a bit, and then added "Yes... yes. Mr. Otto spoke of you often."

Unaware of any previous meeting, Lucy asked, "Have we met before? You said I've grown."

"Pictures, kiddo. Conrad liked to show you off around here. Walter has been here longer than most. He's seen a lot," Stan told her.

Nodding in response, Lucy walked with care through a wide opening that led them into a large hall filled with paintings of funny looking farmers and a rather large one trimmed in gold with a group of men in a tiny boat. "What is this place? Are we the only ones here?"

"There aren't as many as there used to be. The Countess has seen to that," Stan told her. "We are a special group. Everything will be explained over dinner. Walter will show you where you can rest up until then."

The steam bot touched the front of his head and bowed formally. He seemed different from the bots she's grown up around. "Follow me, Miss Ducit, if you please." He led her to a staircase and informed her that it led up to the *Great Hall*. Once there, Lucy understood where the

'Great' part came from. The room was enormous. Filled with statues of warriors and princes, and paintings of kings from ages ago. It was as if time had stopped and preserved all that was there.

"Was this a museum once?" Lucy asked.

Walter opened his arms from his waist outward, "Welcome to The New York Metropolitan Museum of Art. In its heyday, it was a glorious sight."

Lucy continued to follow Walter through huge corridors beautifully mastered by skilled architects and engineers of a bygone era. At the end of the corridor, the pair entered another large room.

"This was Mr. Otto's favorite room. I think this would be sufficient for you as well. It was called Gallery 305: Medieval Art. Mr. Otto was fascinated by this particular forgotten time."

Lucy looked around the room at the paintings of castles, men in armor from head to toe, and various weapons. The most wondrous sight, though, was up at the front of the large room. Reading the faded writing beneath, she discovered it to be the choir screen from the Cathedral of Valladolid and a balcony with the large Byzantine painting. The shadows danced across the ceiling making for joyous wonders. It was already apparent that Walter liked to share his knowledge, and this looked like a perfect opportunity.

"This building was called the Metropolitan Museum of Art, Miss Ducit. Gallery 305 was an original room and then it was expanded from to what we have here today. The people would hold grand parties here called The Met Gala..."

Lucy held up her hand to interrupt the lesson. "What did Stan mean by 'There aren't as many of us as there used to be?' And why did 'the Countess see to that?'"

Walter stood perfectly still. For a moment, Lucy assumed he had malfunctioned. She tapped him on the forehead. "Walter?" she said. He then spun to his left to leave and said, "That is not my lesson to teach."

"Then whose lesson is it? When will I get answers?" Lucy called after him as Walter exited the Gallery.

Lucy plopped down onto a marble bench between two sets of armor, each holding long swords. "What were you hiding, Gramps? Who are these people?" she said aloud, before sighing heavily.

"We are called the Synod of Reaping, and Conrad was hiding your birthright."

Lucy sprang to her feet and turned to defend herself from a man who had seemingly just appeared behind her. "You people have really got to stop sneaking up on me!"

The older gentleman stepped into the light. He had a soft smile surrounded by a salt and pepper beard. His ebony skin was wrinkled and worn, but he seemed to have aged well. He wore a fedora hat, and a worn pair of flight goggles decorated with a brass dragonfly sat on the brim. He radiated dignity and honor and stood before her with his hands clasped in front of him. "Forgive me, Miss Ducit. My name is Gerard Hamilton, and I am the one that sent for you. Conrad and I were some of the first of our generation to realize that we possessed the gift. For over forty years, there was no one I trusted more than him, and he trusted me. That's why he left his diary with me. I assume you received it?"

Lucy nodded her head and patted her backpack.

"Good. He said you would be one of the few people able to figure out how to open the enigma box. In your free time please look over it - learn from it. It will not only act as your guide for what we do, but it will also give you more insight into your grandfather," Gerard told her.

"My guide to what? Who are you people?" Lucy asked.

"We'll get to that." Gerard sat down on the bench and patted the seat next to him. Lucy sat down on the seat, keeping her eyes on him. "Have you read any of his diary yet?" he asked.

She shook her head, "Not really. I found this address from the papers being sent to me and I've been on this wild trip trying to figure out what's going on."

Gerard smiled and leaned closer, "Then I will leave with this: We are a group of special people. People with the gift to end the tyranny that grips this world. Read your grandfather's words, hear his voice in your heart, and know his life and passion. When you come to the dining hall, I'll try to answer more of your questions. You'll get the chance to meet the others as well." Gerard slowly got to his feet with a low grunt. "I don't move as fast as I once did." He gave her a wink and slowly walked away.

Lucy watched him until he was out of sight down the long hall. She opened her dirty backpack and pulled out the diary. "Alright, Gramps. Let's find out what you were up to," she said with a sigh.

She opened the diary and read the first entry dated 12 October 1994:

"Today, I discovered who I really am. I met a man who opened the doorway not only to my past but to my future as well. His name is Dr. Gerard Hamilton, and like me, he is a Reaper. I know what that is now. I will try my best to keep accurate records to further educate others that will come after I am gone."

Lucy read that first page and felt a wave of emotion come over her. She thought to herself, "I can relive your life through your words, Gramps." Wiping a solitary tear from her eye, she added, "I could have helped you..."

Lucy turned the page. The next entry was dated 17 October 1994:

"In only a week, I have seen great evil. The world is headed for dark times if we cannot stand as one against Ruina Baxter. As we search for others like us, we are constantly being harassed and threatened by men in masks. Gerard said these men work for Ruina. She has a personal army being built under the noses of everyone, a multi-million-dollar company, and now has announced her intentions to run for President of the Unit-

ed States. We must shed light on this. The country and possibly the world must know what kind of woman she is before it's too late."

Lucy closed the diary and put it back into her backpack. She mulled over the words she'd just read in her mind, "So, the Countess started all this back in the 90's? How is that possible?"

She sat there in silence for a few moments before deciding to take a look around. Gallery 305, now her room, was enormous, and filled with relics of the medieval era. At the back of the room was a set of doors clearly made by someone other than the original architect. She opened the doors and found a simple area with a bed, dresser, and some pictures hanging on the wall. There was a small frame hung with a pho-to of Conrad and Lucy, with an inscription that said, 'My world.' On the dresser sat a strange looking little black box. Plain and uninviting, it was nothing like the enigma box Conrad had made. It had white letters across the front that said, "iHome."

"What an odd little device. I wonder what it does?" she thought as she leaned closer to inspect it. Noticing a smaller part sticking out from the top, Lucy pressed a button and the smaller device lit up displaying the word 'Autoplay.' Suddenly a rush of sound flooded the room as in-struments, and a screaming man rang out. Lucy grabbed her ears and then started to slap at the device to smash it, or at least turn it off.

"Conrad loved his rock music. I believe that was *Staind*," Stan said laughing as she leaned inside the doorway.

"I don't know what that was, but it was not music!" Lucy exclaimed.

"Have you had time to look around? Conrad loved this room, he said it helped him think," Stan said.

Lucy nodded her head. "There are a lot of gorgeous things here, I never knew the world could be so beautiful. Did you know my grand-father long?" she asked.

"Conrad and I knew each other for an eternity, or so it seemed. I was there, in the distance, when he married your mother and father, and then again when you were born. Conrad was one of my best friends." Stan smiled trying to hold back tears. "Come on. I'll show you his favorite piece of art."

Stan held out her hand and led Lucy through the gallery. They passed wondrous pieces, bright and beautiful; they're full of life. The pair stopped in front of a small bronze statue simply titled 'Dancing Girl.'

"This little girl reminded Conrad so much of you. He said he could see the same bubbly personality in her. He made sure nothing ever happened to this piece."

They both looked to each other as Lucy's stomach rumbled loud enough to echo through the hall.

Stan shook her head and smiled, "It's time for dinner, kiddo. We gather in the lounge on the second floor. You'll get to meet the rest of the group. Come, I'm sure you're hungry for answers, and maybe some food, too." Stan gave a little wink and tugged Lucy toward the door.

The pair left Gallery 305, and walked to an elevator taking them to the second floor. The doors opened to reveal a set of chairs on a platform suspended by chains. "We only have enough electricity to power the smaller devices and tools. We had to modify the elevator system a little," Stan explained.

They strapped themselves into the chairs and then used the chains to pull themselves up to the ascending floor. "Oh, my God! I never expected this," Lucy said to Stan as she took in the sight before her.

Dozens of small brass and glass bots were scurrying about, all carrying tools of various shapes and sizes. The smell of food instantly caught Lucy's attention, and suddenly a pang tore through her stomach reminding her how long she'd been without food.

"I knew you were hungry," pointing to Lucy's stomach, "That thing is a bit of a snitch," Stan said while laughing at the growl that had erupted again. Sweet smells of fresh fruit, baked bread, and the smell of crisp pork invaded her senses all at once. As they entered the lounge, Lucy's eyes were drawn to the lines of wooden tables, each with six chairs around it. Most of which were empty. Two tables at the front had people already sitting and talking, with a third partially filled. As Lucy and Stan came into view, all eyes fell on the pair, but Lucy couldn't help but feel they were mainly on her. A round bot on rollers wearing a chef's hat and a square name badge that read, 'Flo' came whirring up to Lucy. Skidding to a stop, it stood there tapping a pencil on a notebook.

"What does it want?" Lucy asked.

"Flo oversees the kitchen. She just wants to know what you want to eat," Stan informed her.

Lucy raised an eyebrow. "Anything?"

Stan gave a nod. "Anything. Flo is very resourceful."

Lucy thought for a moment and then said, "Grilled cheese, please."

The little Flo Bot beeped and buzzed and headed for what Lucy assumed must be the kitchen. Stan reached down and grasped Lucy's hand as she led her to the others. She gave a small squeeze of reassurance and whispered, "You're with friends here."

They approached the tables, and she noticed Gerard smiling at her, preparing to speak. "Please, take a seat. I want everyone to go around and introduce yourselves. This is Lucy, and she is Conrad's granddaughter."

A murmur of voices started stirring around the tables as a man who looked to be in his thirties stood. His olive skin tried to hide several scars down his arms, but Lucy's eyes were drawn there first. He had a rather large gun strapped to his back that was covered by a brown leather vest that fit the contours of his shoulders nicely. "Hi, Lucy. My name is Jaso Hamilton, and I'm Gerard's son. We will help you find your way."

Next to Jaso was an older man, in his mid to late fifties, who pushed away from the table to reveal a remarkable type of wheelchair. His hair was silver with traces of chestnut streaked through. Twirling a spanner wrench in his hand, he dropped it into a side pouch like a cowboy holstering a pistol and said, "I would stand to do this, but the Countess took my legs in an ambush by the Davarti. I'm just a tinker now. You need something made or fixed, come see me, James Jordan."

Across from James, a young man started to stand. At first, Lucy could only see the back of him, and she didn't mind what she saw. He pushed his chair under the table and turned to face her. Lucy felt her heart race out of control while her stomach filled with butterflies.

"Careful, dear, you're blushing," Stan whispered to her.

Lucy couldn't help herself. Here stood a tall, handsome guy that appeared to be close to her age. His blue eyes seemed to burn into her very soul. He took his hand and brushed his dirty blonde hair back out of his face.

"Hi, Lucy. My name is Micah Jones. I haven't been here very long myself, but I can tell you these people will help you if you let them, and so will I."

Several others stood and said their names with a little about their stations here, but Lucy was still thinking about Micah. He was beyond beautiful and caught her heart in a way she never expected. She wasn't accustomed to her body feeling this way when looking at someone.

A skinny kid with ripped jeans and a faded Yankees hat plopped on his head backwards, stood. "What's up, Lucy? My name is Billy, main thing is to stay clear of my projects. I don't like peeps messing with my stuff, ya know?" Billy waved his hand. "Is she even listening to me?"

"Lucy, you okay?' Stan asked her with a nudge.

"Huh? Oh, yes, he's fine... I... I mean. I'm fine," Lucy said as she searched for the exit.

Flo emerged from the kitchen with a golden brown grilled cheese. "Take a seat, kiddo. Food is here, I think you're getting light-headed."

Flo sat the plate down for Lucy, the bot whistled, and then a door opened in the front. Out came a small bottle of soda held by a mechanical arm.

"Thank you, Flo," said Lucy. The little bot gave a bounce and returned to the kitchen.

"I know you have questions," Gerard said. "We will try our best to answer them. We want you to understand fully who we are, who you are, and what we are meant to do."

After a few bites, Lucy placed her grilled cheese back on the plate. "Okay, let's start with that. Who are all of you? I know your names, but who are you? What does all this have to do with my Gramps and me?"

"We are the Synod of Reaping," Gerard explained. "We reassembled in the early nineties. We existed before then but fell apart because our ancestors did not know how to work as a team. They felt that they were alone in their mission, and that this this feeling was unnatural. Communication over large areas wasn't as easy then. So, the Reapers of old felt they were unclean, or evil themselves, and ended up disbanding."

Satisfied she was following, Gerard continued. "How much do you know and believe from the Bible? Do you know the story from John, Chapter Eleven, about Lazarus?"

Lucy thought for a second. "Yes, he had died, and been dead four days when Jesus raised him from the dead. That's one of the more well-known miracles from the Bible, I believe."

Stan nodded her head, "But there's more to it than that. Most people stop when Lazarus walked out of the tomb. What happened after that? Where did he go?" she asked.

Lucy looked puzzled. "I don't know. You never hear of anything past that."

"When a person dies, the Angel of Death comes to claim his prize. His name is Azrael. When Azrael takes the person's soul there is an essence left behind in the body – a gem," Gerard explained.

"So that's where the shadow gems come from. That slime ball, Martin, at my local memoriam helps with those. The Countess needs them for something," Lucy said.

Gerard tapped his nose, "Exactly. These gems hold the power of life over death. The angel had already taken the soul of Lazarus and was still inside his body forming the gem when Christ breathed life back into him. This caused a conflict. As Azrael was forced out, he left a piece of himself inside Lazarus's gem. Vowing one day, he would reclaim his prize. The Countess uses these gems to fuel her power."

Stan joined in again, "That is where we come in. The priests saw him raised from the dead. They knew the people would turn from the Pharisees and the priests would lose their positions and property if they started believing that Jesus really was the Son of God. These five priests set a plan to murder Lazarus, and eventually Jesus. All of us are in the bloodline of those five Pharisee priests. They hired a man to kill Lazarus and subsequently set out to betray Jesus."

Lucy tried to understand, but she still had questions. "Okay. Does that make us bad people for what our ancestors did?"

"No, no, not at all. That is just why we carry the curse of the Reaper," Stan said. "We have the ability to harvest the shadow gem from a person - to put the soul to rest." She put her arm around Lucy. "This is a lot to take in, kiddo. It was for all of us. We can help you, but first you have to accept your own destiny."

The others slowly started to leave. Each Synod member had a job to do. Each one was an important gear in the mechanism they called family. Lucy needed more answers, but more importantly she needed her Gramps.

5 Aerofall Industries

It was just Lucy, Stan, and Gerard left in the lounge. The little kitchen bots were busy cleaning tables and sweeping the floor as Lucy looked around at the enormous, empty space.

"How do you stay here? Doesn't it get lonely?" she asked.

"We are a family here. And I, for one, never had much of that on the outside," Gerard said. "I tried. I lived what I thought was the perfect life. I met my wife in college and I loved her more than I knew I could. We were married, and soon our daughter followed. We knew trying to start a family and staying in school was going to be hard, but we believed we could conquer anything."

The fact that she didn't meet his wife or daughter sunk in for Lucy. "You had a daughter? What was her name?"

"We named her Emily. She was the best of both of us. My wife, Alyssa, was so beautiful, so innocent. We thought all was right in the world. I had just taken an internship at the biggest and most successful company in the world concerning bioengineering. I loved my job and was good at it. That was, I did love my job until something inside of me drove me to investigate some secret files of restricted research. This research detailed the process of harvesting shadow residue from the recently deceased and The Countess feeding from it."

"You worked for Aerofall Industries? And what happened to Alyssa and Emily? Why aren't they here?" she said, only then thinking better of it. Lucy looked at the ground, "I'm so sorry, Gerard... That was rude of me."

Gerard hung his head, "I worked for Aerofall until I discovered Ruina Baxter's true intentions. How she could hide herself in plain sight for so long is beyond me. She had the world convinced she was the answer to all our problems. She threw her hat into the ring to become the first female president and won it in a landslide two years later."

Stan told her, "Aerofall was the leader in bioengineering in the 1990s. As CEO of the company, Ruina had free reign over what research was carried out and how it was done."

"When I left the company, I met Conrad. We were both drawn to the power of Aerofall, and we bonded over that. The lab techs caught me snooping around the research, so now Ruina knew who I was, and she could sense the Reaper inside of me. I had to distance myself from everyone, so meetings had to be done in secret. She had already threatened my family at that point; I didn't want to endanger Conrad, too. I vowed to try and stop her from taking anyone else," Gerard explained.

"She took your family?" questioned Lucy. "I don't understand."

"It wasn't like it is now. Ruina didn't have supreme power. She had to work in secret, and anyone that posed a threat to her and her research... well, they were met with tragic accidents." Gerard wiped a tear from his cheek, sat up straight in his chair and cleared his throat. "We tried to live in secret, away from danger. I was wrong and couldn't protect them. I let my guard down. Emily had just turned sixteen and wanted a book for her birthday. She wanted to study mechanical engineering and help me and Conrad. I went to a bookstore in town and was seen by her Talfair, he sensed the Reaper inside me and followed me. Ruina sent her soldiers in and killed them while I was away with Conrad. I found them with a note written on the walls in their blood. It said, 'all Reapers are destined to fall.'" Gerard lifted his eyes to Stan. "Jaso was just a baby and luckily was with Conrad and me. It's because of these things that she must be stopped."

Lucy placed her hand on his. "I am so sorry. That must be so hard to bare," she told him. "You said you both were drawn to Aerofall. How so?" Lucy asked.

"That's the power of the Reaper. It's inside all of the descendants of the five priests," Stan explained.

"I think it will be easier to explain in the history room. Come, you'll want to see this," Gerard said as he stood and extended a hand to help Lucy out of her seat.

The trio walked down several dark hallways and into a large room to the west.

Inside the history room were relics spanning multiple generations. A mannequin stood in a glass case, dressed in full armor dated of the twelfth century. Down the aisle stood another mannequin wearing camouflage fatigues and a helmet from World War II. The group rounded a corner and Lucy was startled by a disfigured statue.

"What happened to this guy? He's wearing a Davarti uniform, but something is wrong. Why is his skin so gray? And the veins in his face are black!" she exclaimed.

"This is how her soldiers came about. They were a side effect of her research at Aerofall," Gerard told her.

"I've never seen one with their mask off. Do all of them look this way?" Lucy asked.

"He's dead, dear," Stan told her. "Reanimated flesh of the people the Countess harvests Shadow Gems from."

Lucy gasped and covered her mouth in shock, "The Countess's Soldiers of the State are dead? How? How do they move and fight?"

Stan paused. "The Countess uses the essence of Shadow Gems to transform the dead into her soldiers. By absorbing their souls, she can continue her life, and she controls their bodies."

Gerard placed her hand in the bend of his arm and led her to a board hanging between two frames. "This is a summary of what we know. A timeline of sorts, if you will. In 1993 I discovered what the Countess was doing at Aerofall. Ruina announced her candidacy for President, and she promised change. She promised a plan that would put humanity on its proper course. What she wasn't telling everyone, though, was that the course she was preparing was world supremacy, with her at its head. When she won the presidential election in ninety-six, she did as she promised. Poverty was at an all-time low, the economy was on an upward spike, and homelessness was becoming unheard of in major cities. That's when she introduced the Soldiers of the State, the Davarti, to control violence and crime. The soldiers patrolled areas that police were too afraid to go into, and this made the people love her. Ruina made such an impression on Congress that they agreed to let the people vote on allowing her to stay in office for life, not just two terms."

"I read in my grandfather's diary that she already had the army before she ran for president," Lucy said.

"She did. But not the numbers she has now. She rounded up the homeless from the bigger cities: San Francisco, Chicago, New York and the like, and they became her Davarti. Her personal security at Aerofall. She couldn't reveal them until the right time. I was a twenty-year-old intern. I had to tell someone what I had found. I met Conrad as he was starting his freshman year in college. Once Ruina started collecting the shadow gems from the bodies of her victims, though, it triggered the Reaper inside of us. That's what led your grandfather to Aerofall and our paths to cross. I had already been dealing with the curse and found it refreshing to share this with someone else," Gerard told her.

"You keep talking about this curse of reaping or having the Reaper inside you... What is it exactly?" asked Lucy.

Stan pointed to the board where a Bible verse was written in bold, blue letters. "John Chapter eleven," she said. "This is the story of Lazarus, which we were talking about earlier. All the Reapers are ancestors of the five priests that witnessed this miracle and ultimately had Lazarus murdered. Azrael had claimed Lazarus. When the priests had him killed, they took the prize from the angel again, denying him his revenge. This infuriated Azrael, as they had cheated him of taking the life of the one that had already been stolen from him once."

As she spoke, Stan had retrieved a scroll from a drawer of a large chest. As Stan unrolled it, Lucy could see beautiful hand-drawn images.

"This parchment was painted by a priest in the Orthodox faith approximately thirty years after the miracle of Lazarus in Bethany. It documents the confrontation between Azrael and the five priests. He gave them the chance to repent but as they dropped to their knees, Azrael laughed and mocked them saying, 'I do not grant forgiveness. You mistake me for the Son of God.' He cursed them to an eternity of being lost. He told them, 'I cannot sentence a man to Hell, but I can make your journey on earth long and tedious.' He touched each man on the forehead shouting words in Hebrew. Each priest was transfigured into a key, and as they landed in the sand, Azrael named them: Knowledge, Love, Time, Death, and Life. These five keys hold the power to unlock the resurrection miracle inside the shadow gem left in the body of Lazarus. These keys are what is needed to stop the Countess and make her mortal again."

Lucy looked closely at the paintings of the five keys, it was heavily worn and faded. She couldn't read the language, but she knew in her heart they were telling her the truth.

"If Gramps trusted you, so do I."

"Ruina has learned to use the power of the original Shadow Gem to keep herself alive. The power of resurrection and death all in one. She also holds Lazarus' remains, making it difficult to access his Shadow Gem. We must unlock the power inside of his gem to stop her. This will satisfy Azrael, and should rid us of this curse," Gerard added.

"So, when we get these keys it will undo this funky mojo inside the Countess and stop her. Cool! So where are the keys?" Lucy asked.

Stan looked at Gerard then back to her. "That's the problem. We have been searching for them since we learned of their existence with no luck. That was fifty years ago for the ones left here. Others searched long before us. We feel that we are getting closer, but I'm sure the Reapers of the past did as well."

"Conrad was convinced he could figure out their locations using the ancient texts and parchments. He believed he had been close several times. The last time... well, the last time was when we lost him." Gerard said as he lowered his head in respect. "Conrad dedicated his life to the understanding of the ancient Hebrew ways and texts. We have only made it this far because of him and his talents."

"I want to finish what Gramps started, and I think we can do it together," Lucy stated. "Maybe some of his talents, as you call them, rubbed off on me?"

"We?" Stan asked with a raised eyebrow. "You sure about that, kiddo?"

Lucy crossed her arms. "Well that's why you wanted me here, isn't it? Your numbers are low, so you need all the help you can get. Besides, I was the only one who could unlock the enigma box. So yes, we," she said with a twinkle in her eyes.

Gerard cleared his voice in an awkward tone, "Well... yes. Yes, that was one reason."

"Then we have work to do," Lucy exclaimed. "We can sort out the other reasons later."

Over the next few weeks, Lucy would be trained in the ways of a Reaper. They would coach her in hand to hand combat and even firearms. A Reaper had to rely on their wit and instincts against the soldiers of the state. They would show no mercy to a Reaper, or anyone that the Countess wanted dead for that matter. Lucy had to be ready.

6 The Training

The training room was on the fourth floor of The Metropolitan. The room had been cleared with only a few columns for support. The white marble floor seemed to shine and shimmer beneath their feet. Jaso oversaw Micah and Lucy's training in weapons and defense.

"Lucy, have you ever fired a pistol before?" Jaso asked.

He was met with a resounding, "NO! Why would I ever have needed to... well not until now."

"Well, then today is your lucky day!" he said. He opened a black case that sat on the table beside him. The case was old and worn with two brass latches. Inside the case lay two gorgeous pistols nestled into a pillow of deep red velvet. Each one had a matte black handle, trimmed in bright brass. A crimson red barrel and lower ammo chamber were perfectly crafted.

"Those are beautiful!" Lucy exclaimed. "Almost like a work of art. Did you make them for me?"

Jaso took the weapons from their case and twirled them on his fingers to turn the handles toward her. "They were Conrad's. He and James created these beauties. Only fitting they go to you now."

Lucy took them in her hands. The handles felt as if they were designed to fit the palms of her hands. The weight was perfectly balanced, not too heavy or too big. She traced the craftsmanship of the barrel with her finger, looking closely at the marks from years of use.

"Now for you, Mr. Jones. I have something special for you as well." Jaso clicked a small button on the table. A door slid open in the floor, and a mannequin wearing a harness lifted through the floor. "You have had your training in firearms, and have proven yourself with a long rifle and short-range pistol. Now you will learn the ways of the Sentai Blade."

The harness held two swords crossed on the mannequin's back. The handles were shiny black, with brass compressed in rings around it. The hilts were pure titanium. Jaso took the harness and secured it around Micah. "You have to be comfortable with the blades. They will be your first line of defense and your most lethal line of offense, so they should become a part of you. You need to be able to handle these as if they were an extension of yourself."

Micah adjusted the harness, twisting and pulling until he could easily reach the handles that were just behind his shoulders. He slowly unsheathed the Sentai Blades and brought them out in front of him. The blades were bright blue with black markings running the length of each. Lucy had a silent thought that Micah's blades matched the blue of her hair.

"What does this say?" Micah asked pointing to the inscription on the blades.

Jaso took one of the blades carefully in his hands and turned it to reflect the light. "'Live life as a champion, and live forever.' It is the mantra of the Reapers." Jaso handed the blade back to Micah. "You will need to practice sheathing and unsheathing them as quickly as possible without injuring yourself. So, I suggest starting out slowly. We don't want you losing your head." Micah stood there with his mouth open rubbing the back of his neck as it registered that decapitation was a possibility.

"As for you, Miss Ducit. We need to start with the basics." He went through the process of loading, unloading, and holding the pistols correctly. "You need to practice this until you can do it in your sleep. An empty firearm is a useless firearm." Jaso took a small remote from his belt pouch and pressed a button. A freestanding frame about thirty yards from them sprang from the floor. A bull's eye was painted in the center. "Let's see if you can hit the target," he said. "Hold your arm out in front of you. Good, now look down the barrel and line up the sight at the end with the center of the target. Breathe in through the nose, out from the mouth. Concentrate."

Lucy lifted the pistol with both hands in front of her body. "Not with both hands!" Jaso snapped. "That's why you have two pistols."

Again, Lucy lined up the pistol with the target. This time she did so with only her right hand, though it was slightly shaking. "When you have the target, gently squeeze the..." A loud, rippling shot rang out, piercing the air. Micah ducked down behind the table as Jaso finished his sentence. "...trigger."

"Did she hit it?" Micah asked with a laugh. "Five bucks says she didn't!"

Jaso took the pistol from Lucy, checking the safety and then laid it on the table. "Let's go see."

They approached the target and Lucy let out a squeal.

"She hit the target!" Jaso exclaimed. "I'll collect that five bucks later, Mr. Jones."

The target had a single bullet hole three inches from the top of the bullseye. "With practice, you will hit the center without giving much thought to it," Jaso told her. "Always remember the safety after firing! The last thing we need is you shooting yourself, or one of us accidentally."

Lucy nodded her head, still smiling with pride that her first shot had actually hit the target.

In the several weeks following, Micah and Lucy would train every day. He would help her with her aim as he was learning the feel of his Sentai Blades. One day, Lucy asked him, "Jaso said you had your training with guns. You any good?" She pulled a pistol from her thigh holster and handed it to him. Micah took the gun and slowly moved in close to her. He trailed her body gently with his fingers from her cheek down until he reached the other holster. Lucy took a deep breath as Micah pulled the other pistol. In one move, he not only had the firearms spinning, but both guns were blaring. The blast of gunpowder lit up the room like fireworks in the dark of night. The lingering smell of blast powder burned her nose with a stinging odor, but she hardly noticed it in the air. He stopped firing, and both arms dropped to his sides, smoke swirling up from the pistols. In the blink of an eye, Micah moved behind her lowering the guns back into her thigh holsters with a twirl on his fingers.

She could feel the heat of the steel warming her legs and the warmth of his breath on the back of her neck as he leaned in and whispered, "Check the targets."

She tried to keep herself stable and finally caught her breath and composed herself. Lucy walked to the target area. "Looks like you're at fifty percent. Six targets, twelve shots. I see one hole in each. I thought you'd be better."

With a smug grin, Micah told her, "Look closer."

Lucy walked closer to the first, shaking her head, then moved to the second to see all targets had two holes overlapping. He hit every bull's eye twice, almost in the exact same place.

"Wow!" she said and she started walking back his way slowly clapping her hands in approval.

"Those felt really good in my hands," he told her.

Catching her off guard, she stuttered, "What? Wh... what did?" Her cheeks flushing a dull red as she gripped her shirt.

"The pistols. Your Gramps had good taste in firearms," he said pointing down to her holsters.

Lucy quickly collected herself. "Oh... Right! The pistols," she said releasing the breath she was holding in. "They are beautiful, aren't they?"

She turned away from him and face-palmed. "Stop acting like a stupid school girl!" she mumbled under her breath.

"Did you say something?"

"I said you copped a cool twirl," she said closing her eyes. She mouthed the word 'stupid!' as silently as possible.

The two finished their routines and began to tidy up the training room.

"How is the research going from the diary?" he asked, pulling a chair from the table. "Are you getting any closer to the location of a key?"

"I'm meeting with Stan and Gerard tonight. I have a few questions about some things I found," she told him. "Gramps talked a lot about his first days here and finding Gerard, but I've not seen much about the keys yet. They said he believed he had been close, though."

"I hope that through that diary, you and your grandfather can set things right. This place is great, but I would like to be free someday," he told her.

Lucy gave him a slight smile, "Maybe they can make sense of some of this stuff," she said. "Because most of it seems like gibberish."

7 Road Trip

Later that night in the Great Hall, Lucy was admiring some paintings from the fifteenth century. She found one that caught her attention showing a group of people. One looked like Christ himself, with a man kneeling in front of him offering a key. Could this be a sign? As she was mulling over her discovery, Walter summoned her. "Miss Ducit. Mr. Hamilton and Ms. Stanley are ready for you in the library."

Lucy followed the little bot into what once was the Thomas J. Watson Library. Now, it was home to the scholars of the Synod of Reaping. The library was a huge room, wider than it was long. Tables were in rows and Lucy counted at least ten chairs around each one. The walls were lined with bookshelves taller than she was, with ladders on wheels to move around and reach the books. Seated at a table near the center Lucy saw Gerard and Stan.

"Lucy! So glad to see you. I hear your training is going quite well. Are you getting the feel for those pistols?" Gerard asked as he stood and offered her a chair.

Lucy just gave a nod.

"Looking good, kid. Those pistols seem as if they have always been yours," Stan added with a wink. "Haven't seen much of you since your training started."

Lucy sat down and dropped her backpack on the table. She pulled Conrad's diary from the backpack and slid it to the center. Several different colored bookmarks were sticking out from the pages.

"I think you were right about Gramps tracking the first key. He had been back-tracking a lot of details for a while," Lucy said as she opened the diary and read:

"'Entry date: Saturday 28th October 1995. I followed up on a lead today. It brought me to the beautiful city of Atlanta, Georgia. The city is buzzing because their baseball team is close to winning the World Series. With all the people on the streets, it makes it easier to cover my tracks. The first key definitely is the Key of Knowledge and it's guarded. By what or by whom I do not know. That explains why my calculations keep coming up wrong from the parchments. It may be moving. I need to find this first key so we can be closer to stopping Ruina Baxter before she pulls us all into darkness.'"

Lucy looked up and said, "That is all he wrote on that date, and he didn't write again for eight days."

Stan seemed to drift off into a memory, "I remember that Atlanta trip. He didn't mention anything about the key. He just said it wasn't what he thought."

Lucy flipped through the pages, "How long was he in Atlanta? Do you remember?"

Stan thought for a moment. "Six days, I believe. Maybe seven?"

"So, if he didn't record anything in the journal for eight days, we don't have anything to go on. No clues as to who he met with, or where he went or what went down," Gerard said. "What would have kept him from writing down what he found?"

"He did scribble something on the opposite page. It's just one word 'Blackfall'. What do you suppose that means?" Lucy asked.

"It means we are going on a road trip," Gerard told her as he looked to Stan. "You ready for this?"

Stan just lowered her head and groaned. "The Pallidus people scare me. No one should be that pale, and don't get me started on those gray eyes! Whatever you do, don't stare. They hate to be stared at."

"Atlanta is so far away. How are we supposed to get there, especially unnoticed?" asked Lucy.

Gerard smiled and stood, "The Synod have many hidden resources. We can thank Conrad for most of them. Go fill in Micah and you two be ready in a couple of hours. Meet us on the roof. We will be in Atlanta before morning."

LUCY FOUND MICAH IN the workshop with James working on some new tinkers. When she walked in, she was struck silent by the sight of Micah shirtless, and a little dirty as beads of sweat ran down his back. She followed each one as it followed the contours of his muscles. As she leaned on the doorframe she found herself drifting off to a place she believed to be heaven. She saw him turn and speak to her. Angels voices arose filling the air with joyous sound. The corners of her mouth would not deny a smile and she didn't want to stop it. He called her name and she felt a jolt race throughout her body. Starting at her head and swirling around her heart. Her knees weakened as she her him call her again...

"Lucy! You in there?" James shouted as he tossed another wire nut, bouncing it off her forehead.

"I came to... I was sent to see Micah... GET Micah, I mean. Gerard said we are going on a road trip. We are to meet him on the roof," she said trying to regain her composure and rubbing her head.

"Well, if you guys are going out, you will need your armor," James told them.

Micah had joined them now. Both, he and Lucy look at each other with confusion. She filled him in on the road trip.

"Well, come on. I know they don't want to wait on you two," James said as he led them to a set of doors. "Lucy, yours is in the left room, Micah yours on the right. I hope it works. I didn't know you would need them so soon."

As they stepped into their dressing rooms, they found a bag hanging on the wall which reminded Lucy of a something you'd see at a Cleaners. Each bag had their names on the outside along with the

S&R symbol of the Synod. Lucy unzipped the long zipper down the front of the bag and swelled up with excitement "This is beautiful!" she squealed.

Micah spoke next. "James, you have outdone yourself. This is far better than the gear I was practicing in," he said as he stepped out.

It was clear Micah was pleased. Looking in the mirror, he noted how the new armor looked. A black vest with silver studs circling the sleeve cuffs above his biceps. It was sleeveless for mobility, so he could easily access his swords. The gloves had the same silver studs in two lines from the back of his hands leading up his forearms on the black leather gauntlets.

"This is my favorite part of the whole thing," Micah said as he flipped the hood over his head and slid it just above his forehead. "It makes my eyes pop, yeah?"

James gestured for him to lean down so he could check something. He grabbed the hood and pulled it down over his face, thumping him right in the head.

"You can see through the material, you numbskull! Your hood is the most important part of your gear. You guys are new, and if the Countess or her men can identify you, she will hunt you down. Or worse, kill everyone you hold dear."

Micah nervously tugged at the hood to pull it down further. "Well, when you put it that way."

"Lucy! You okay in there?" James shouted.

The door slowly opened, and she stepped out.

"Are you sure this is for me?" she asked.

"You look stunning..." Micah said breathlessly, his eyes wide.

She had on a green leather corset with several straps buckled around it, over a white mesh blouse that sat under leather scalloped shoulder plates. Her hood was made from the same type of material as Micah's, but she didn't need to rely on hiding her identity as much since Martin had already informed the Countess of who she was. Her boots were a lavish forest green laced up over her knees. Black mesh trousers were tucked inside the boots.

James beamed with delight. "There's only one thing missing!"

Lucy grabbed at her corset, "I hope it isn't something else to wear, I'm sure it won't fit in here," she said as she blew a big gust of air from her lungs.

James tossed her a belt, "I thought you might like this one, it belonged to Conrad. I just modified it to your measurements as best I could."

Lucy caught the belt in her right hand and saw custom holsters dangling down. She squinted her eyes and said, "What is that written on the belt? Crimsunrain? What is that?" she asked as she started to fasten the belt around her waist.

"That is what he called them, the pistols. They are Rainmakers. In his hands, nothing was left standing; his enemies would be rained upon by his wrath," James told her. "One last thing, for both of you. You may need these in the underground." He gently opened a box that sat on a nearby table. Inside, they saw four metal orbs the size of lemons. "These are light grenades. They won't harm or damage anything but pack a punch of light like a small sun. Be sure to have your goggles down if one of these babies goes off," he told them. "The Pallidus people stay away from light. This will be enough to paralyze any of them in a dicey situation. Now, head on up to the roof. Don't keep the team waiting!"

As they walked up the spiral stairs to the roof, Lucy asked Micah, "Have you ever been on a trip for the Synod before?"

Micah shook his head, "Not one that could involve fighting and danger. I was sent on a supply run once, though. I have a talent for staying hidden pretty well." He stopped her and placed his warm arms around her shoulders, looking deep into her eyes. "Don't worry; I got your six."

Lucy shot him a strange look of confusion. "What exactly is my six?"

Micah laughed. "It means I've got your back. It's an old military term. You can count on me to watch out for you."

"Then I will have your six, too," she told him.

Opening the door to the roof, they could see a huge airship. The balloon that carried it was almost the size of the Met. Glorious guns could be seen lining the sides from portholes the length of the ship. The front of the ship was adorned with an enormous metal skull painted black. The brass outlining the cabin shone as brightly as the sun against the deep mahogany wood. A long walkway led up to the bow of the ship where Gerard was standing. He was dressed in his full body armor, and enough steam power coursed through the pipes to give him super-human-strength. He looked to be thirty years younger. He still had his 'business as usual' vest on, but the armor added mechanical muscle that aided his arms and legs to move freely with him.

The gears turned, and pistons pushed steam out of the vent holes as he waved to the duo to come on board. "Stop delaying, we need to head out," he told them. As they got closer, they noticed he was wearing a top hat made of aged leather with a set of flight goggles strapped across the brim. The handle of a massive sword could be seen over his right shoulder. "Glad you two could grace us with your company. Come on board and strap in. We take off in ten minutes."

As they boarded the ship, a familiar voice rang out. "Cabins are below, store your gear and report back to me. I will need your help with the steam propulsion."

"James? How did you get here so fast?" Lucy exclaimed.

James laughed and said, "Who else would fly this bucket of bolts? The Countess took my legs not my brains! This is no ordinary chair."

As he made his way from behind the wheel box, they noticed his chair.

"Wow! Your wheelchair has legs, too?" Lucy blurted out with amazement.

"My chair can sprout legs like a spider. While you two were lol-lygagging around, my chair and I came up the back of the building," James said with a chuckle.

"Oh, that's not all it has," Micah told her. "Show her, James."

She could see almost all of James's teeth from the smile he produced. He looked like a proud parent showing off his baby. James lowered his goggles. Turning a knob on the left, he pressed the pressure switch on the right, and suddenly the chair was fully armed with miniature guns on both sides and a tank like cabin where James was tucked away behind reinforced plate glass and brass.

"Wow, it's a mini tanker!" Lucy was impressed.

With the turning of another knob, pressure was released and the chair transformed back to a mobile unit, and James shouted, "Five minutes to lift off!"

Lucy and Micah were stepping through the doorway leading to the cabins when Stan came into sight. "Separate cabins. Away from each other," she said with a raised eyebrow and squint of her eyes.

"Yes, ma'am," they both said in unison and turned in different directions.

Depositing their bags, they hurried back topside to help James. "Micah, you handle the thrusters. Wait for my mark. Lucy, when I give you the signal, pull that lever to give us lift off." He positioned himself behind the wheel and waved his hand. "Now, Lucy!" he shouted.

Lucy gripped the lever and pulled it down releasing hot gas into the balloon. The ship jerked and was soon airborne. "Twenty percent, Micah! Forward!"

Micah turned the dials of the thrusters, and a rush of air escaped from behind them, pushing the ship forward.

"We will be in Atlanta in a couple of hours," James confirmed. "Rest up. If I need you..., well, I shouldn't need you."

With the ship effortlessly sailing through the air, Lucy walked to the bow and held onto the railing. Her bright blue hair whipped behind her head and swirled to the front of her face. She closed her eyes and took a deep breath. She had the feeling of being free.

"First time flying?" Micah asked from behind her.

"Is it that obvious?" she answered.

Micah folded his arms on the railing and leaned forward taking the air in through his nose. "This is the second time for me. It does seem to put you into a peaceful state up here. As if nothing is going on down below. They came to pick me up in The Silvertooth. That was my first time."

Wrinkles formed on Lucy's forehead as a confused look spread across her face. "The Silvertooth?" she asked.

Micah stood upright. "It's the name of the airship. If you look inside the skull's mouth, it has a tooth of pure silver. The others are just iron and steel."

"Hey, you two! Before your 'on top of the world!' moment hits, we need to go over some things," Gerard called up to them.

They walked down and saw the others standing together waiting on them.

"Bout time you got here. I'm a cripple, and I can move faster than you two," James spouted.

"If you're here, who's piloting the airship?" Micah asked.

"Humph! It's called auto-pilot. What have you been teaching these kids?" James muttered, looking to Gerard.

Gerard stood in front of them and said, "First thing: this is a recon mission, only resort to violence if they initiate it. According to Conrad's diary he came here sixty-three years ago to find information on the first key. A lot could have been forgotten, and in that period of time I'm sure they've changed a bit. Second: I feel he did find something and that's why his journal was sketchy and blank for a while. We go in, we ask our questions and we hope to God we find something we need."

"Third: Most importantly, stay together. These people don't take too well to surface people. After they went dark, their sense of humanity seemed to vanish. They don't trust many," Stan added. She laid a hand on Lucy's shoulder, "If you're not ready, we can go in without you."

Lucy took a deep breath. "No. I'm a part of this now. It's what Gramps would want for me, I know it."

"You were all he'd talk about for a while," James said. "He was impressed with how you turned out..."

Gerard shot him a look to say, 'stand down'.

"Impressed? How?" she asked.

"What he means is Conrad knew how much potential you had and how well you would fit in with the Synod and his work," Stan told her.

"How much longer till Atlanta?" Gerard asked to change the subject.

"I'll go check the gauges," James said as he headed up to the control panel. "One Hour!" he soon announced.

"I think I'll go to my room and try to clear my head before we land," Lucy told them.

"Good idea, sugar. I'll come get you when we hit the Atlanta airspace," Stan said with a smile.

8 Atlanta

Lucy sat down on the bed, resting her head against the wall for several minutes. She leaned forward and opened her backpack, pulling out her grandfather's diary to read a little more.

'Journal entry dated 5th November 1995. My trip to Atlanta was uneventful, mainly because I can't remember any of it. I told the others nothing because I didn't want them to know I had failed... again. I did find an unusual object in my hand when I woke up behind the Varsity. I'll put it in the pouch in the back cover. I must start my search over again. There has to be something I'm missing, but what?'

"Back pouch?" Lucy asked aloud. She flipped to the back to find a leather pouch that was sewn into the back cover. One single snap button held the lid closed. "Well, Gramps. Let's see what you found."

She popped the snap and opened the flap. Searching inside, several items fell out, one that brought Lucy to tears.

"I remember this day," she said as she held a picture in her now trembling hands. "This was the best birthday I ever had. Everyone was so happy, even Gramps." The date on the picture was November 22nd, 2047. Lucy's eighth birthday. She tilted the photo back and forth to activate the holographic images so she could see the people laugh as the candles on a cake were being blown out. "It was also the last time I saw my parents," she thought.

Lucy wiped the tears from her face, shook her head to try and regain her composure, and placed the picture in her pocket. "What else is in here?" she asked with a sniff. A media brochure with Atlanta on it caught her eye. She opened it and began reading. "Wow! This was actually a tourist attraction? That big rock with the old army men on it has been overgrown with moss and hippie realists for ages!"

A whistle rang out followed by James's voice. "Ten minutes to land-ing. Steady as she goes. Atlanta is in sight."

Stan knocked on her door. "It's time, hun."

Lucy folded the faded brochure and put all the contents back into the pouch. She checked her gear and headed up to the open deck. The once great metropolis of Atlanta lay spread out before them. Buildings that once touched the sky were now crumbled heaps of debris. She no-ticed a huge open-air stadium lined with seats, where at one time ath-letes would have competed in spectator sports for the glory of the peo-ple, like gladiators of Rome did in centuries past. The stadium was now, apparently, home to thousands of migrants looking for work.

They made a pass around an extremely large building with a golden dome that once housed diplomats, and was now home to Viceroy Zacheous Atwood, overseer of the south. Viceroy Atwood had been in power for over three decades, sitting atop his golden throne, stuffing his face with every type of food imaginable while his people starved and killed just to survive. To say the Viceroy was a hefty man wouldn't do his size justice. From pictures Lucy had seen of him, he had constant sweat pouring from his brow. She'd heard tales of him barking orders from his seat of power as servants scurried to keep him dry. Then he would call for more ale and his 'between meals' snacks. Viceroy At-wood was a horrible man, but he was also the lesser of the cruelest of all the Viceroys put in place by the Countess.

The area known as Underground Atlanta came into view. Lucy saw a sign that read: 'Welcome to the dirty South; you'll never leave.' An-other was painted saying, 'This is the ATL' and 'Above ground bound.' A building was painted bright red with a set of large white eyes, but the white leaked from the eyes as if it had dripped before drying.

Lucy looked down at the ground, "Do you think they know we are here?"

Gerard simply answered, "Yes." Then he grabbed her and shoved her toward the deck floor. Before she could ask anything, a loud boom shook the rafters of the Silvertooth. "That was a warning shot. We have to signal below that we mean no harm."

Gerard stood and walked to the bow of the ship, removing a single white handkerchief from his pocket, waving it above his head. "We just want to talk!" he yelled toward the ground.

A large clump of debris started to move to one side, revealing a landing pad underneath. As the Silvertooth touched down, several figures appeared around a square doorway that led down into the Underground. The landing plank touched the ground, and the passengers disembarked into the realm of the Pallidus people.

Stan placed her hands on Micah and Lucy's shoulders. "Whatever you do, don't stare at their eyes. They hate it and will take it offensively. You don't want to see an offended Pallidus..."

As they approached the doorway, a rather large being blocked their path. "What business do Reapers have in the Underground?" he asked.

Gerard held his empty hands up and stated, "We just want to talk to Dadeag. Is he available for council?"

"Dadeag Blackfall no longer leads the Underground people."

"We are aware of this, but he was leader of what was the Blackfall Crew sixty years ago. We need information from a meeting he had with Conrad Otto," Gerard added.

Again, the larger Pallidus spoke. "We will see if Lord Jeramine will allow it."

"Dadeag's son leads the Underground? I thought he died," said Stan.

No answer came from the large Pallidus as they turned and led them down the walkway. As they walked, Lucy could feel people watching them. Eyes fixed and piercing through them. "I don't like this," she whispered to Micah.

"Just stay calm and don't make any sudden moves," he told her.

They were led down the makeshift roads lined with former businesses.

"Did the city sink underground at some time?" asked Lucy.

"No, not quite. This was a major shopping center at one time. People would come from all over to shop and dine in the fabulous Underground Atlanta. After the riots in 2020, most people decided to leave the city, not wanting to fight the Countess and her new army. These are a group of people that stayed, and they have resisted the Countess for decades. They moved underground to stay out of sight," Stan told her softly.

The group stopped in front of a large archway leading into part of a building. The windows were shattered, but the columns still stood. The spokesman turned to Gerard. "Wait here. If he wishes, he will summon you."

Gerard gave a nod of his head and watched him walk away. They waited. After what felt like an eternity, a much smaller figure approached them.

"I am the humble servant of Lord Jeramine Blackfall. I am to escort you to him." The servant bowed and turned to lead them.

Large slabs of concrete had been moved to form tables and seating in a circle that surrounded a large throne-like chair in the center of the dimly lit room. Several pale figures occupied the surrounding seats with their eyes fixed upon the visitors. Sitting in the center on the throne was an unusual looking male. He was just as pale as the others, but his body was covered in tribal looking tattoos.

"Why do Reapers approach the Darkened Throne and ask for the Lord's father?" asked Jeramine in a deep and booming voice. His arms were very muscular, which left Lucy a bit concerned.

Gerard stepped forward and took to one knee. "We seek only to ask questions, my Lord. We are here on a mission of information."

Jeramine stroked his long, braided beard. "I will grant you council with Dadeag. Though, you will find information has been lost to his mind. I cannot guarantee your mission will be fruitful."

Gerard stood and bowed his head, "Thank you, my Lord."

Jeramine waved his hand, and the small servant reappeared. "Follow him to Dadeag," he said motioning toward the group.

The servant bowed to his lord and led the group away. "Dadeag's mind betrays him," he informed them. "He has not been the same in some time. His mind grows as dark as the world around him. That is why Jeramine took the throne."

"How long has he been like this?" asked Stan.

"Ten, twenty years. No one cares to keep up with you if you are no longer Lord of Pallidus." The servant stopped and pointed to a dark doorway on the left. No guards, markings, or anything signified that it held a person that once controlled the Underground. Just a sad and dark existence for a once brave and loyal leader. The group entered slowly to find only a bed in one corner and a single chair in the center. Dadeag was standing behind the chair... talking to whoever he imagined was in the chair.

"Dadeag?" Gerard asked.

The old man stopped his babbling to look at him. "Gerard! My old friend! What brings you to the darkness?"

Stan leaned closer, "You know him, Dadeag?"

He smiled, "As well as I know you, dear Kathleen."

"Always the charmer, Dadeag," she said with a smile. "We need information about a meeting you had with Conrad many years ago. Can you help us?"

"Ah, Conrad. He sought the Keys," he said with a cough. "How does he fare?"

Stan hesitated, but said, "Conrad is gone, Dadeag."

"Aren't we all?" said the former Lord.

"Yes, we believe that's why he came to you," Gerard told him. "Can you tell us about your conversation with him? Can you remember?" he asked.

Dadeag slowly walked from behind the chair toward them. As he inched his way into the dim light, Stan noticed something.

"Oh, Dadeag. What did they do to you?"

The elder Pallidus hung his head. "When you are no longer Lord, you are no longer fit to bear the markings."

His skin was heavily scarred and torn. The very people he led had removed the royal tattoos that a Lord of the Underground bore. Dadeag tried to cover himself from the shame with his bare hands. "They said I was unfit... ME! ...unfit. I ruled this realm after the riots took our homes, our families, and our livelihood! I am still fit to..." A coughing fit prevented him from completing his speech.

Gerard and Micah grabbed the old man before he fell to the floor and eased him into the chair.

"Please, we need to know about your meeting with Conrad. What did you tell him about the keys?" Stan asked him softly as she took his hand.

Dadeag's eyes fixed forward. "Ask this one." His crooked finger stretched out, pointing straight to Lucy. "She holds all you need to know. Conrad poured all the information into her." He started to laugh and cough manically. "Conrad Otto! Master Tinker and Reaper extraordinaire! HAHAHA! He thought he could play God himself."

Lucy started to back away from them, "What is he talking about? I don't know anything about the keys or what he's saying!" She turned to run and bumped into one of the guards that had heard the commotion. As she hit the floor, the light grenade that James had given her fell from her bag and went off.

The guards covered their eyes and screamed, "Protect the realm!"

In their panic the guards sounded the alarm alerting the others to danger. Dozens were on their way to defend against the Reapers.

"Dadeag, please! Tell us what we need to know about the key!" Stan shouted.

"The eyes of Lee tell all! The eyes of Lee need to fall!" Dadeag shouted as he leaped to his feet. "Living in the dark allows me to see what others have to hide." He pointed back to Lucy. "I see you! I see what you have to hide!"

Micah grabbed Lucy, "We need to go! Now!"

They ran as hard as they could, Stan and Gerard not far behind. They could see the light from the outside. Just as they approached the opening, the giant Pallidus guard blocked their path. He drew his weapon and fired. Micah stepped in front of Lucy with the Sentai blades crossed, deflecting the rounds into the chests of two oncoming guards to the side. Micah slid between the guard's legs to get behind him, slicing at his legs as he passed. Just as the guard spun around to fire upon Micah, a snap was heard, and Stan pulled the barrel of the hand cannon back toward the face of the guard. A bright flash, a loud boom, and he was no more. Behind Stan, Micah saw Gerard punching one after another. A turn of the piston knobs on the armor and his strength increased to that of ten men. Left, right, left. Fist after fist smashing into the oncoming Pallidus army.

Micah pulled his own light grenade and shouted, "Goggles!" He tossed it past Gerard and into the onslaught that was coming for them. In a flash, all the Pallidus were on the ground, writhing in pain. "Come on! Now's our chance!" shouted Micah.

James already had the Silvertooth ready for takeoff. "I heard the ruckus and figured you might be in a hurry." As the last one boarded, he yelled: "Now, Lucy!"

With a pull of the lever, the ship was airborne. "They're getting ready to fire on us!" Gerard shouted.

James barked commands to his crew. "Lucy, keep as much steam coming as possible. Micah, keep your hands on that wheel, we need to keep steady. Stan, lower the back shields and hurry! Gerard, come with me to man the guns!" Without hesitation, everyone fell into place. Just as Stan got the shield in place, a mortar shell rocked the airship. Lucy lost her balance and fell to the deck hard.

"You, okay?" Micah yelled from the helm.

Lucy nodded and continued to pour steam into the balloon.

James and Gerard each controlled a gun mounted on the sides of the ship. "Aim for their gun towers!" Gerard yelled. "We just need to get away."

Like synchronized thunder, the guns blazed in a shower of death. The towers couldn't take the punishment, and they exploded under the pressure. A huge plume of black dust and debris erupted from the Underground.

"Steady as she goes, Mr. Jones. We're going home," said James.

Lucy let out a sigh of relief and felt a pinch in her elbow. "I must have fallen harder than I thought," she thought to herself as she checked for blood. "No! This is wrong!" she shouted. "I can't be..." she said as she fainted to the deck.

9 Old Memories, New Facts

When Lucy woke up, she was in her bed back at the New York Met.

Stan was there with her. "How are you feeling, hun? You had us worried."

Lucy slowly raised herself up, rubbing her head. "I had the strangest dream. I hurt my arm on the ship and when I looked at it..." She felt the bandages covering her elbow. "Tell me it was a dream! Tell me I'm not crazy!" she screamed as she tore at the bandage on her left elbow.

"Lucy, stay calm. It's okay, kiddo. I promise," Stan told her, trying to steady her hands.

Lucy ripped the outer cloth from her wound to reveal seven brass staples holding a deep cut together.

"What did you see?" asked Lucy. "What did you see in my elbow?"

Stan sat on the bed still holding Lucy's hands, "Let's wait for Gerard. Just lay back down and relax."

Tears started to form in Lucy's eyes. Her breath was shallow, and her cheeks were flushed with anger and panic. Stan could feel the heat radiating from her. With a deep glare and in a serious no-nonsense voice, Lucy said, "Tell me what you saw, or I swear I will rip these staples out and see for myself. I have to know."

Stan pulled Lucy's hands gently down to the side. "Okay. I will tell you, but you must know we weren't trying to keep anything from you. We were waiting for the best time."

Lucy locked eyes with her. "When is the best time to know what? What's wrong with me?"

Gerard knocked, and opened the door as he walked in with James right behind him. "How are you feeling, Lucy? You have your color back I see," noted Gerard.

"I'll be a lot better once I get answers," she said.

Stan's brow was deeply furrowed with concern, but she gave Gerard a nod.

"Please close the door, would you, James?" asked Gerard. "Now, Lucy. What do you remember about how your parents died?"

Lucy threw her hands in the air. "I don't know what that has to do with what's wrong with me! Why can't I get a straight answer in this place?"

Gerard held up his hand. "Patience, Lucy. I'll get to that. Now, what do you remember?"

"I remember Gramps picking me up from Academy and taking me for ice cream. I knew something was wrong because we never had ice cream before we went home," she recalled. "We just sat there, not much was said. We just ate the ice cream and started home."

"Did you go home?" Stan asked with her eyes fixed on the floor.

Lucy concentrated hard, trying to get a clear picture. Her eyes grew wide, chest heaving, short of breath. "No..." she stammered. "No, we didn't!" Panic started to set in again. "We came here. Why did we come here? Why couldn't I remember that before?"

"That's the elixir I gave you to help calm your mind, and to help heal your body. It also opened some of the doors you had closed in there," said James. "We just have to help you find those doors."

"You must understand. We are here to help you," Gerard told her. "First, what you saw inside the laceration on your elbow is called a Pneumatic Action Piston."

"Why is it inside me?" Lucy interrupted.

"This is the most important part. Remember, stay calm," he stated. "When your parents were killed by the Davarti, you were in the car, too.

The Countess wanted all three of you dead... and she succeeded. For the most part."

"My parents died when they crashed their car when it malfunctioned because of faulty bots at the factory. I was at school," she muttered as her arms crossed her body and she began to rock back and forth.

James raised his hand. "I planted that memory of the classroom."

Gerard spoke again. "Your mother, being the child of a Reaper, was herself a Reaper. She helped us and Conrad fight the forces of the Countess, just as you are doing now. They knew they had to protect you because your mother's identity had been compromised. They were taking you to a safe house when the steamer cab rolled over a trigger mine in the road. Someone leaked the location, and the Davarti Soldiers were waiting."

With her hands now firmly embedded in her hair, Lucy asked, "Then why wasn't I finished off? Why leave a liability behind?"

"They would have if they had found you. Being a reanimated dead foot soldier doesn't leave much room for intelligence, kiddo," Stan stated.

"Your mother was killed instantly by the blast. You and your father were thrown from the cab. You were seriously injured, fatally injured, in fact, but your father held out hope. With his body riddled with shrapnel from the mine and the car, he managed to hide you and make a last stand to distract the soldiers," continued Gerard.

"That doesn't explain how I'm alive or why I have this... thing!" Lucy exclaimed as she pointed to her elbow again.

"You are evidence of a brilliant mind!" James stated. "Conrad Otto was the best at engineering steam intelligence. I can only hope to be half the man he was in that workshop. He told us he had a bad feeling about the trip to the safe house. He went to check on you but he was too late. He found what was left of the cab and his family. The fear that they had taken you had begun to set in when he heard a noise from behind some bushes. You were cold and still, but he brought you here. We tried to tell him you were gone, to let you go, but you were all he had left."

Stan took Lucy by the hand. "You were given a second chance at life. Somehow Conrad knew you were destined for great things. Things that would save our world."

"I can't be whatever you think I am. I was just an average girl, living an average life, with less than average friends. I have never been in a fight. I'd rather run. I can't do this."

"It's not a matter of if you can or can't," Gerard added from the foot of the bed. "It all comes down to if you will or won't. Your grandfather thought you would. Was he wrong?"

He crossed his arms, "You are a miracle that modern times can't duplicate. Help us finish what Conrad and I started."

One by one, they shifted their gaze to Lucy. Her body was shaking from fear and confusion. "I'm scared," she said.

"We all are," Gerard told her. "But we don't let that define us. We are our own destiny. Our paths take us where we need to go. We just have to choose if we are going forward, standing still, or falling back."

Lucy sat on the edge of the bed that Conrad had slept in for countless years. She ran her fingers up and down the sheets, twirling the fabric. She looked around at the items that once meant something to him. She almost felt like he was sitting there with her, trying to comfort her.

"Who else knows about me and my condition?" she asked in a satirizing tone.

"Just the ones in this room, chick. The others think you are sleeping off pain meds," Stan told her. "It's your secret to tell."

"Good," Lucy said. "Let's keep it that way. At least until I can handle who or what I am myself."

The others all nodded in agreement as Lucy reached for her backpack on the table. She pulled Conrad's diary out and opened the back flap.

"I know what Dadeag told Gramps," she said holding up the old brochure. "We need to go back to Atlanta. We're going to Stone Mountain."

"Are you sure?" questioned Stan.

Lucy's lips were quivering as she answered. "No. But Gramps wanted this. He wanted me to carry on his work." She wiped her eyes and took a deep breath. "If I didn't at least try I would never forgive myself."

10 Stone Mountain

That night, Lucy met with the group in the library. Everyone sat around the table with her in the middle.

"Dadeag kept screaming about the eyes of Lee. He said the 'The eyes of Lee sees all. The eyes of Lee must fall.'" She slid the Stone Mountain Park brochure to the center of the table. "One of the figures carved into that mountain is Robert E. Lee of the Confederate Army. I believe the riddle was talking about this carving," Lucy pointed out.

Gerard let out a loud sigh, his fingers rubbing his temples, "We have to go back to Georgia, but with us barely escaping the Pallidus they will be looking for us, and this time they won't be so nice."

He clapped his hands onto the desk as he stood, "I'll go alone. I can't risk any of you."

Jaso spoke up, "I don't think so! You left me here on babysitting duty last time, and you needed my help. Walter can watch over the others while we are gone."

"If the Countess finds out where we are going, she'll send her army or possibly even show up herself. We could use Jaso, Gerard," Stan added.

Gerard's lips pinched together like he needed to spit. "Ah! Fine, but we can't just head back down there. We will give it a couple of weeks to die down."

Stan gave a nod to Jaso. "We ready for this?"

"We'd better be," Jaso said ringing his hands together. "Because, you can bet, they will be."

OVER THE NEXT COUPLE of weeks, the Reapers laid out a strategy for Stone Mountain. They gathered as much information as they could about the area, and readied supplies and gear onto the Silvertooth. Lucy was learning what it meant to be a Reaper, their duties, abilities, and responsibilities. To be one of the few people left that could save her world from a tyrant was overwhelming. At night, Lucy would walk the halls of the Met looking at what the world used to be like or she would lie awake and read Conrad's diary. It gave her glimpses inside the life of the man she had previously only known as Gramps.

'Journal entry, 1 December, 1995. This year has opened my eyes to more wonders and miracles than I could ever imagine. I am a Reaper. It took me a while to admit that. Not many know of us, and that is a good thing. If word got to Ruina Baxter who had the power of the Reaper, she would stop at nothing to destroy us. The worst part is that she has convinced this nation, and possibly the world, that she can bring change. She has announced her candidacy for President of the United States. If she succeeds there, I fear the world will fall to her power.'

Lucy closed the journal and lay her head back on the pillow. "I can't remember a time when she wasn't in power. I wonder how the world was before her?" she thought.

The next morning during breakfast, Jaso and Gerard were talking about the trip.

"Are they ready?" Gerard asked. "We can't risk losing them to the Countess, so we need them prepared. I'm sure she will try to beat us to the key."

Jaso took a sip of his coffee and wiped his mouth. "They need experience under their belts, but they are learning fast."

Lucy walked over to their table with a plate of waffles, "So, when are we leaving? I think the Underground has cooled off by now. We don't want to risk the Countess finding something before we do."

The men looked at her in bewilderment. "What? Do I have syrup on my face?" she asked, standing in full gear. Her bright blue hair pulled back, showed a face of determination that would not be deterred.

"Have a seat, Lucy. Let's talk," Gerard said as he pushed out a chair from the table with his foot.

Lucy sat her plate down and took a seat. "I've been reading more of Gramp's journal. I'm starting to see what you guys are doing, your purpose behind this mission. I've read some of the stuff you've had to endure, and it's truly awful. I was born under the rule of The Countess, so this is all I've ever known. I now realize this world could be a lot better. It *used* to be better, and that's why Ruina Baxter needs to be brought down."

Jaso held up his cup of coffee as if he were about to make a toast. "I couldn't have said it better myself." He and Lucy looked to Gerard.

"Well, what else can I add?" he said tossing his hands up in the air. "Let's get that key!"

Lucy smiled and picked up a naked waffle, "It feels good to have a purpose!" She folded the waffle in half, dipped it into the puddle of syrup on the side of her plate and took a big bite.

Gerard laughed and asked, "Is tomorrow soon enough for you, ma'am?"

Lucy smiled "Well if that's the best you've got, it will have to do," she said, flashing a wink. Jaso almost spewed coffee all over them. The trio shared a laugh and finished their breakfast.

That afternoon, Lucy was talking to James and helping him ready the Silvertooth for another long trip down south. "So, you helped Gramps do this to me?" she said while pointing at her almost healed elbow.

James put down his spanner wrench and wheeled right up to her. "You say that like it's a bad thing. Do you see me as some kind of freak, or just inferior because of this chair?" he asked sternly.

She stumbled backward, shocked by his response. Knocking over some boxes, spreading nuts and bolts all over the floor. "No... I never...

that's not what I was saying," Lucy said as she folded her hands in front of her.

James smirked, "Then what were you saying?" he asked. "Do you consider yourself less human because you have some parts inside you that you were not born with?" He didn't give her time to answer, "To answer your question, though, yes. I helped Conrad on the most brilliant project I have ever had the honor to be a part of. Your grandfather's mind worked like the machines he invented; flawless. We took you from the brink of meeting Azrael in person, to a healthy living little girl."

"How much of me is still... me?" she asked poking around at her stomach.

"It's all you!" he exclaimed. "This chair is me! Is it the path I would have chosen? Hell no. It's the path that we were handed, and I'll be damned if I'm going to roll over and fold because it wasn't part of my ideal plan. I'm different, and that's not something to pout about. None of us are perfect. None of us are exactly where we need to be or want to be. That's why we keep moving forward, because we already know what's behind us. Keep pushing forward. Fight. Live. If not for you, do it for Conrad. He believed in you."

James wheeled over to the bench and picked up a screwdriver, trying to hide the tears in his eyes. "I fell into a deep depression after I lost my legs. I felt like half a man. I was sure people would look down on me or treat me like I was helpless. One day your grandfather came to me and asked if I had given up. If I was just going to give up and let Ruina win? Before I could say anything, he answered for me. He handed me this screwdriver and told me I wasn't going to give up. Conrad encouraged me that I wouldn't be confined to this chair forever. He designed this chair, and it gave me a purpose. It gave me my life back; your grandfather gave that to me."

Moments passed and with tears staining her cheeks, she wrapped her arms around James. "Thank you."

"For what?" he asked.

"For helping me see what my eyes weren't willing to," she told him. Lucy saw a side of him that helped reveal more of the secret world her grandfather was a part of. These people were *a* family, and now they were *her* family.

Like most nights, Lucy sat alone in her room inside Gallery 305. This was when she felt closest to Conrad. She would look at the picture from the back pouch of the diary and let her mind drift to memories of him. She knew tomorrow was going to be dangerous. Something inside her felt the Countess would be there. She pressed the button and the screaming voices of heavy metal blaring from the iHome strangely soothed her to sleep.

THE NEXT MORNING THERE was a knock at her door. "Almost ready! Come on in if you want!" she shouted.

The door opened, and Micah stepped in. "Micah! I thought you were Stan!" she exclaimed spinning away from him to finish the buttons on her shirt.

"I told the others I would come get you," he said with his eyes fixed on the floor and shoulders slouching forward. "I wanted us to have a moment to ourselves."

"Why do I get the feeling you don't want me to go?" she asked him.

"I don't want to see you get hurt. Do you really think you are ready?" he asked her.

She walked slowly toward him, her eyes fixed on his. "Isn't that why you have my six?"

Micah tried to hide the smile that was forcing its way onto his face. "I'll always have your six."

She held her hands out in front of her, palms up. Micah placed his in hers. Slowly, he leaned in to gently kiss her. She clenched her fingers tightly and gave a twist of her wrist forcing his arm behind his back. With her index finger pressed to his head like a gun she whispered into his ear, "The only time I won't need you, is when you are needing me." She released him and smacked his forehead playfully. "Now come on, we have a key to find." She grabbed her bag and walked out. Micah took a deep breath, and straightened his gear before flashing a smile.

"She is something else. Something else indeed," he said as he ran to catch her.

On the roof, they were boarding the ship when Jaso stepped in front of them. "If you love birds have the kissing out of the way, can we go now?"

Lucy's face turned blood red, and she tried to answer, "We... he... Well..."

"Love birds? What are you talking about?" Gerard punched Jaso in the arm. "Leave them alone; we have work to do."

They readied the ship and took to the air. Lucy closed her eyes and rubbed the scar on her elbow. Being back on the ship felt awkward now. The air pushed through her hair bringing goose bumps to her skin.

"Is it as good as the first time you flew?" Micah asked as he walked up beside her.

"I could get used to this," she answered. "The feeling of freedom up here is wonderful. I just hope there's not a surprise like last time."

"Last time?"

"Oh, you know, the Pallidus. I hope this trip is a little smoother," she stuttered.

"Maybe when we get the keys and end all this, we can fly somewhere. Just the two of us," he told her.

Lucy felt her heart skip a beat. She tried to swallow the lump that formed in her throat. "I would like that," her head hung low. "But I have some issues I need to deal with before any of that happens."

Micah took his finger and angling her head up to face him. "We all have issues, that's why we're here in the Synod. I know how to be patient, though. When you're ready, I'll be here for you."

Lucy was smiling on the outside. 'If you only knew the truth, you wouldn't be wanting to wait,' she thought.

The Silvertooth broke into Atlanta airspace, and James' came over the loud-speakers. "We will be at Stone Mountain in ten minutes. All hands-on deck and keep your eyes peeled for those blasted Davarti."

As the huge rock formation came into view, Jaso turned a dial on the side of his goggles and zoomed in on the mountain-top. "Too late, James. They're already here! Lower the shields and get ready!"

The large plates shifted into place with ease.

"Gerard and Jaso, man the rickshaw cannons and wait for the signal." A loud boom was heard as the Silvertooth was rocked by mortar fire. "Now, boys! Show them the way out of here!" James shouted from the main deck.

The rickshaw cannons were rapid-fire weapons that dealt massive amounts of damage. Mounted on the side of a swivel platform with two wheels, they could turn almost in a complete circle. Gerard gave a thumbs-up through the hull to Jaso, and the pair opened fire. Each round fired from the rickshaw cannon was the equal in power to twenty short range shotguns, with a rate of fire at three rounds per second. After the shells were fired, they split into smaller rounds, each with explosives inside. The smaller rounds pierced the armor of the Davarti Soldiers and exploded on impact spewing the undead in all directions. Another mortar was then fired from the ground barely missing the right cannon.

"That was too close, James! Can you try to make it a little harder for them to hit us?" Jaso shouted.

James yanked the wheel to the left. "Pfft, kids!"

As the right side of the Silvertooth shifted toward the mountain-top, Gerard opened fire again. "Woo-hoo! I love this!" The soldiers fell like dominoes one by one. The troops were thinning out as Stan motioned to set the ship down. Dust and debris swarmed around the ship as it descended. Light as a feather, James guided the ship down.

"Do we even know where to look?" Jaso asked as they readied themselves to leave the ship.

"Dadeag said the eyes of Lee," Stan said. "But how do we scale a mountain with Davarti on us?"

James shifted some levers on his chair. Gears buzzed and whirled, grinding loudly into place. With one last turn, the chair now had eight legs again, like a spider. "I'll get to 'The Eyes of Lee', you just keep them off me."

They formed a line between James and the Davarti as he disappeared over the edge.

"Here they come!" Jaso shouted.

Gerard tightened some of the knobs on his armor and steam rushed down the sleeve chambers. Gears turned, and pistons started to pump warm steam power through the armor. Gerard was once again filled with the power of ten men. With a loud "Rah!" he pulled the sword from his back, and ran straight ahead steam-rolling through the middle of the first group head on. He hit the first one so hard that he turned to dust! One after another, he punched and sliced through them. The second wave of Davarti were flanking from the right.

"Keep a lookout for James!" Jaso shouted. He pulled two grenades from his belt and threw one right at the feet of the oncoming horde. The blast sent the front line flying and as the bodies hit the ground, Jaso threw the second grenade into the middle of the pack. Boom! The second blast cleared a hole, blowing undead everywhere. Jaso pulled two gut-ripper rifles from his back holsters and unloaded into the remaining minions.

"Found anything yet, James?" Stan shouted.

"I'm having a little trouble down here!" he yelled back.

They looked over the edge to see James. He was clinging to the side of the mountain with four legs while the other four were fighting off soldiers, rappelling down the edge. Dangling directly above the head of Robert E. Lee, James had the bubble shield in place for protection.

"There's too many of them," Stan said. "Stand strong; I'll be right back."

Kathleen Stanley was no longer a young woman, but when needed, she could move faster and more agile than most half her age. She ran toward the edge of the mountain, opened her side satchel, revealing a rope that she had tied to an old metal post mounted in the stone. The other end of the rope she attached a small device the size of an apple. She pulled a key out of the device and threw it over the edge.

Three... two... one... The rope swung over the top of James in the direction of the swinging Davarti. Three diamond blades emerged from the device. As it made contact it severed the ropes of the troops, dropping them to the ground below. As it swung back toward James, he moved up and grabbed the rope with one of the arms of the chair. Tearing it free from the rope he loaded the small device into the mini gun of his chair. He fired it at three soldiers wearing steam jet packs headed his way. The bladed ball hit the chest of the first one coming out his back, causing the steam tank to explode. The shrapnel flew back and knocked the other two from the air. "Ha! I was hoping that would work!" James cheered.

Exhilarated, Stan ran back to a better position. "Hang in there, James. I'm going to help."

11 Viceroy Comes

James heard a thud on the bubble shield covering his chair. One of the flyers landed on him and was now pounding away. A shot rang out and a hole formed in the center of the Davarti soldier's mask, spewing undead matter all over the shield. The bullet exited puncturing the steam canister on his back, launching the Davarti like a rocket. James wiped the goo off and saw Stan with a long rifle giving him the thumbs-up from the ledge. Micah and Lucy looked all around finding each member with their hands full as they just stood there.

"We have to help them," Micah told her.

Lucy shook her head, grabbing onto his hand. "We were told to stay here."

"Gerard and Jaso can't hold them off much longer by themselves," he said as he unsheathed his Sentai blades. "We have to help them, or none of us will make it out of here." Giving her a wink he said, "I have your six. I promise."

Micah ran to help Gerard as his armor seemed to be collapsing under the pressure of the steam. The blades sliced through the undead soldiers with little resistance. One after another, Micah cut them down, trying to make his way to Gerard. Suddenly, the ground shook, and a loud shrieking sound could be heard. A rather large soldier with spiked shoulders came lumbering forward holding a ship's side cannon at his side.

"Watch out for that one!" Gerard shouted to Micah. "He may be slow, but that gun is fast."

Micah turned to face the oversized grunt. Steady on his feet, the large Davarti, roared and pulled the trigger, unleashing a flurry of hot ammo at Micah and Gerard. Micah didn't have time to think, his body reacted to the situation. He crossed the blades in front of him as the bullets ricocheted off them. Turning his wrists slightly, he deflected them back in the direction they came from. Knocking the smaller Davarti off their feet, he managed to line it up with the side cannon itself.

The bullets entered the barrel and collided with the exiting ammo causing the cannon to jam and explode. Micah saw his chance. He charged the big guy, swords at his sides. The larger Davarti was still disoriented by the blast of his weapon, tilting and staggering around. Micah leaped into the air planting his feet as he came down into the chest of the enormous undead. The force was so great that it knocked him off his feet, flat on his back. Micah rode him like a surfboard to the ground where he planted both Sentai blades in the giant's eye sockets.

Gerard saw Micah handle himself with ease and it stirred a second wind inside of him. He pushed his armor to its limits, turning the pressure gauges to their maximum. "I hope this works," he whispered to himself. He reached for his sword and found nothing there. Looking around, he grabbed the closest soldier by the ankles, and then he used him as a war club to pulverize the others. Steam rushed from the armor, hissing and buzzing, as the heat rose. Gerard saw the gauges straining to keep up with the power, and yet he pushed on.

Jaso took his dual gut-ripper rifles and locked them together. With the pull of a lever on the side, he was now launching time delayed mortars in every direction. He rushed to his father's side and rained a circle of ticking destruction around them. The remaining soldiers came rushing toward them only to be caught in the blasts of the time delay bombs.

Micah searched for Lucy and saw her with both pistols drawn, backing up to the cliff's edge. Her body was trembling as the tears flowed from her eyes. Three of the Davarti were closing in on her. "Lucy, shoot them!" Micah shouted. "Just as we practiced! Aim for their heads!" She raised the pistols in her shaking hands and aimed at the soldiers. It was hard to see through the tears, and the shaking made her guns move.

"Do not let Conrad's legacy be destroyed. Be brave, Lucy!" Stan yelled.

Hearing her grandfather's name brought her back into focus. She was no longer afraid, no longer trembling. Now she was just angry. They took him from her. Her jaw clenched tight. With her arms straight, she pulled the triggers and dropped two of the oncoming Davarti in their tracks. Bringing her hands together, she fired both rain-makers at the last one. The blast from both pistols at once took the minion's head clean off his shoulders, the body still running until it fell at her feet.

Micah came to a skidding stop beside her. She still had both pistols out in front of her as he listened to her short and choppy breathing. He felt her whole body as it trembled.

"Lucy, it's okay," Micah said as he slowly lowered her arms. "You're okay. Can you hear me?"

She dropped the guns to the ground and wrapped her arms around him. "I was wrong... so wrong," she told him, voice cracking and scattered.

He held his left hand tight against the small of her back and his right was behind her head trying to comfort her, to ease her mind. "About what?" he asked.

"I will always need you," she said. "I will always need you to have my six or seven or whatever it is," Lucy exclaimed, holding him as tightly as she could. Her body felt as though she would drop to the ground if she let go of him.

Micah moved his hands to her face, tilting her head up to look at him. "I am forever your partner in this fight. We will have each other's back, always," he locked eyes with her leaving something unspoken between them.

"Hey, guys!" James shouted from the edge of the mountain behind them. "I think I found something!"

Lucy and Micah just smiled. He closed his eyes and let his forehead rest on hers. "Later?" he asked.

"Later," she replied.

They ran to check out what James had found. Gerard was slowly limping on his left side as he made his way to them. "Is it the key?" he shouted. "Tell me you found the key."

James stopped where they were standing, his chair reverting back to a normal looking wheelchair. He held out his hands, "The eyes of Robert E. Lee." James told them. "The riddle said they see all and they must fall. So, I gave them a little tap with a pneumatic spanner, and they popped right out. The interesting thing is what's on the back of them..."

James was interrupted by a loud, slow clapping coming from the building on the top of the peak. Spinning around they saw the Viceroy, Zacheous Atwood. Sweat was pouring from his rather large head, soaking the collar of his suit.

"How did you make it up this far, Atwood?" Gerard asked. "Did you make your men carry your sorry butt all the way up here? No wonder they looked tired as we beat them."

Micah tried to hide his smile and chuckle with the back of his hand. Stan poked him in the back and gave him a stern look. "Sorry," he told her.

"I will take whatever that is you found in those eyes," the Viceroy said. "The Countess requires it."

"Now you know us better than that, Zacheous," Jaso said with his hands on his hips. "We didn't work this hard just to hand it over to you or to the Countess."

The Viceroy wiped the sweat from his brow as he started to laugh. He placed the handkerchief back into his front jacket pocket. "Don't make me work up much more of a sweat than I already have, Reaper. I promise to kill you quickly, if you cooperate," Zacheous said to them.

"Now, now, Viceroy," Stan said. "Even you aren't that stupid. There are six of us and only one of you. Granted there are five hundred pounds of you, but still... just you."

"That hurt my feelings," he said brushing a hand down his stomach. "I've lost a few pounds." Zacheous began to unbutton his suit jacket, dropping it to the ground to his left.

"Oh, dear lord!" Stan gasped.

"I think I'm going to be sick!" Lucy said placing her hand over her mouth making an awful gagging sound.

"My God, are you even human anymore?" Gerard asked.

"Yes, and parts of me are better than human. These were a gift from the Countess herself!" Zacheous exclaimed as he raised not one, but two sets of massive arms. "Do you like them?" he asked.

Everyone pulled their weapons and took aim at the massive Atwood.

"Oh, you can put away your pesky guns. They have no effect on me any longer. Muahaha!" the Viceroy stated.

Under his coat and suit wasn't the stack of blubber that they thought. The Countess had transformed him into an abomination. Using parts from not only other humans, but animals as well. He possessed the strength of a grizzly bear, the girth of an elephant and the limbs of a silver back gorilla.

"Well, my time is money," he said as he cracked both sets of his knuckles in front of him. "I need what you have." The behemoth charged straight for James. Jaso opened fire with both rifles. He watched as the bullets sank into his skin, but never fazed the Viceroy.

James quickly placed the stone eyes into a locked compartment inside his chair and activated the bubble shield. "Not today, Viceroy! Ha ha! Not today!"

The shield slammed shut just as the Viceroy pushed into him, all four fists pounding the barrier. With a snap, Stan caught one of the massive arms with her whip and gave it a yank.

"You're getting too old for this, Stan!" Atwood shouted as he yanked on the whip's end and sent Stan flying to the ground. He used the whip as a leash and pulled her to him.

Gerard ran to her and sliced the whip's end, "Get back! Get Lucy out of here. We will handle Atwood."

Stan got to her feet and grabbed Lucy by the arm, pulling her to the side.

Gerard gave the pistons one last twist. "Nothing left in the tank," he said. "I'll have to do this the old-fashioned way." He motioned for Micah and Jaso to converge on the Viceroy who was back to pounding on the shield of James's mini tank.

Jaso and Gerard reached Atwood at the same time. Jaso swung as the Viceroy blocked with his upper right hand. As he did so, the bottom right lowered, connecting with Jaso's mid-section, doubling him over at the waist. The upper hand followed, smashing down on his back and slamming Jaso to the ground with a sickening thud. Gerard was just a step behind Jaso and came in with a leg sweep to try to knock him off balance. Atwood was ready for him though, his left lower fist catching him, pinning him to the ground as the upper left arm repeatedly smashed his limp body.

Micah vaulted from the top of a large rock. He struck the Viceroy in the face with his boot as he pulled both blades from their sheathes as he came down. Atwood hoisted Gerard between the two as a shield just as Micah twisted the blades away from him. The razor-sharp Sentai blades barely missed the unconscious Reaper. At once, Atwood sent Gerard flying into Micah, slamming both hard, hurling them to the ground as James opened fire again with the mini guns. Each bullet sinking deep into the putty-like blubber of the Viceroy.

"I told you," Atwood said. "Guns have no effect on me. The bullets just tickle as they go in." Slowly, the Viceroy lumbered to James and pounded on the shield once more, forcing cracks in the framework.

"I have to put some distance between us," James whispered. Looking around, he shrugged his shoulders, mumbling, "I hope this works. All power, forward thrusters!" The mini tank roared and shot forward with a blast straight over Atwood, coming to a stop about two hundred feet away.

"That's it!" Atwood shouted as he spun around. "No more mercy! No more Mr. Nice guy. I want that key, and I'll happily tear you apart to get it!" He lumbered forward toward James.

Lucy nudged Stan, "He's moving slower now." She pointed to the Viceroy, "It's like he is weighted down or something."

Stan moved her eyes from the still motionless Gerard and watched the Viceroy labor and shuffle with each step. Jaso was making his way to his feet, shaking his head trying to clear his mind. Stan shouted to him, "Your rifles! Use your rifles!" She pulled her pistol from the thigh holster and ran toward Zacheous. Jaso pulled both triggers sending a volley of hot lead into the body of the Viceroy. James caught on to what they were trying to do and again opened fire with the mini guns. Each round entered the massive body and started to drag at him. Atwood's knees began to buckle under the weight. He stopped in his tracks and fell to the ground using his lower arms to brace himself.

"You may slow me down," he said. "But you can't kill me! I will find you, and I will break you into..." Atwood's eyes grew large, and they could hear a gurgling sound coming from his throat.

"That's why we can't let you leave, Mr. Viceroy." Micah was behind him with both blades buried to the hilts. He retracted the blades, and the lifeless body slumped to the ground.

Stan stood with Micah, "Take his head so the Countess can't resurrect him." As Micah took care of Atwood's body, Stan rushed to Gerard. Jaso was holding him, "Hang on, Pops. We'll get you patched up." He gently laid Gerard across James's chair, and they headed back to the ship.

Once they were back on board the Silvertooth, and had Gerard strapped to a bed, they headed back to New York. They gathered around a table in the galley. Jaso still had Gerard's armor in his hands. He could see the suit had been pushed too far and was out of power.

"He'll pull through, kiddo," Stan told him. "He always does."

"He shouldn't have been out there," Jaso said. "He's too old to still be doing this." He hurled the armor across the room crashing into the wall with a thud.

James was coming through the door as the armor flew past him. "A little warning next time, maybe?"

Micah spoke up, "Well, what did you find? Was it the key?"

James held up his hand, "Don't get your panties in a bunch. We will look closer at them when we are back home safely."

The group silently did their duties of the ship. Each one dealing with what had happened in their own way; each one hoping what they just went through was not in vain. The group needed a win.

12 Gateway Stones

The Silvertooth touched down on the roof of the Met back in New York, and they carefully settled Gerard into the med bay. As the medical bots began to scan Gerard, the group made their way into the library to see what they had found on Stone Mountain.

"He'll be okay, Jaso. Your dad is a fighter, and I just know he'll pull through." Stan tried to sound convincing.

"I've been so nervous since we landed," said Lucy. "I want to be by Gerard's side, but at the same time I want to know what we found. Then there's another part of me that wants to find the Countess now, and make her pay for this."

"She will get what she deserves," Stan told her. "It's just a matter of time."

Jaso looked to James. "What did you find?"

James laid two stones the size of grapefruits on the table. "It's another blasted puzzle!"

Jaso pushed himself away from the table, knocking the chair to the floor. "So, we aren't any closer than we were?" he asked. "My father is fighting for his life for what? Rocks!?" He stormed toward the door as Stan called after him.

She rushed to the door to catch him. "Jaso! This has to mean we are closer!" she said placing her hands on his cheeks. "We have to believe."

"I wouldn't expect you to understand, Stan. He's not your family," Jaso said as he stormed out the door.

Tears stung Stan's eyes as she watched him head down the hallway back to the med bays. "No, but you are," she said quietly to herself. She wiped her face and returned to the table with the others. "If this isn't the key, what is it?" she asked.

James picked them up and pointed to an inscription on the back of each one. "I think if we can figure out what these say, it will lead us to the key," he said tossing them back to the table.

"Do we have a way to translate?" Micah asked as he picked up one of the stones to examine the text.

Stan looked over the other one. "I've never seen a language like this in any of the archives here. It may not even be words." She handed her stone to Lucy.

"The markings seem to be a part of the stone itself. Not carved into it, but raised from the surface," she said as she rubbed her fingers over the writing. "Do both pieces have the same markings?" she asked as she held her hand out for Micah's stone. He dropped it into her hand. As soon as it touched her palm, the stones began to glow.

"Whoa! What did you do?" asked Micah. "Lucy?" He snapped his fingers in front of her, but she was in some kind of trance.

"Biikousiis Heey-otoyoo Ceesey Hisei' Nonoo hooto," a voice rang out from Lucy.

Everyone stayed very still and quiet.

"It has been many moons since a chosen has come forward. We will speak in your tongue. You must go to the long mountain of Colorado, there by the highest moon the one woman will see."

The stones dimmed, returning to normal. As they fell from Lucy's hands, the loud boom on the table snapped her out of it. "Why are you all staring at me?" she asked scanning their shocked faces.

Stan jumped to her feet, feeling Lucy's forehead and cheeks. "You aren't aware of what just happened, kiddo?"

"Yeah, we were talking about the markings on these rocks, and then you guys spazzed out on me," she said irritably.

Micah picked up the stones, squinting hard at them. "When you held both stones you went into a trance of some kind," he said. "You were speaking, but it wasn't you... speaking..."

Stan grabbed Lucy's hand, "We can find the key! It told us where to go!"

"Yeah, where to go. HA!" scoffed James.

Micah kicked him under the table. "Good try, kid. Can't feel anything there, remember? Just chair."

"Why did it work with me and not James? Or any of you?" questioned Lucy.

"The voice called you a chosen. It spoke about a long mountain in Colorado. We will have to search the archives to figure out which mountain that is," James said. "There are a lot of mountain areas there. We have our work cut out for us."

Stan added, "It said once there, the one woman will see by moonlight. I'm sure the one woman is you, and by moonlight, you will see the key."

"I can't wait to leave!" James said in a more excited tone that he had ever used. "I haven't felt this close in years!"

"Do we wait for Gerard to get back on his feet?" Micah asked.

Stan shook her head, "No, I will explain everything to Jaso, and he will come. Gerard should stay here. He will need all the rest he can get." She clasped her hands in front of her, "Besides, we still need to figure out exactly where we are going."

James picked up both stones again. "Lucy, see if they have anything else to say." He handed them to her and everyone held their breath.

Lucy held them in her hands, giving them a little shake. When nothing happened, she tried to ease the tension. "Sorry. Maybe they are just starter stones?" she said with a chuckle.

THE NEXT MORNING STAN went to check on Gerard. "I can't stand to see you lying there like that. You were always the strong one. You have to get better." Tears streamed down her face, dropping onto the dark gray blanket covering Gerard. "You need to get better not just for me, but for our son as well."

She heard a creak in the floor behind her in the doorway. Stan spun around to see Jaso staring at her. "Our son?" he asked. "My mother was killed along with my sister by the Countess. What, did you and my father have an affair?"

Stan walked closer to him. Jaso held up his hands to stop her. "Just answer the question."

"No, we did not have an affair. Gerard loved Alyssa more than life itself, he still does. She and Emily were his world," she told him. "When he lost them, he was devastated. It drove him mad in his pursuit of the Countess. You were the result of a love he was afraid to share. He felt it disrespected the memory of what he and Alyssa had. He pushed me away."

"That doesn't explain how I was told I was her child and not yours. Who else knows this?" he asked.

Stan wiped her tears again. "No one knew except for Conrad. It was even before James came into the Synod. Everyone else that was here at the time is gone. We felt it would be better for you. He felt that way. His love for Alyssa was greater than anything I could ever give him until I gave him you. I love your father, and for one night, he loved me."

Jaso walked past her to his father's bedside. He took his hand. "Why didn't you tell me this? Why keep me in the dark?" he asked.

Stan placed her hand on his shoulder, "He didn't want you to be disappointed in him."

Jaso turned to face her, his face riddled with confusion and anger. "So, he rather I live in a lie, and think that my mother is dead to protect his image?"

Stan tried to respond, but he pushed past her, leaving her to watch him storm out.

LUCY WAS BACK IN HER room listening to Conrad's heavy-metal music on the iHome device. She looked at herself in the mirror. "The stones called me a chosen. Chosen by whom?" she thought. She looked to her elbow and ran her finger across the bandage.

A knock at her door had her jumping. "It's open!" she shouted.

Micah came in with a plate in one hand and two sodas in the other. "What's this?" she asked.

"Grilled cheese. I thought we could share one and talk," Micah said with a smile.

They sat down at a rickety little table. Each had a half of sandwich and a soda.

"Flo makes the best grilled cheese."

"Actually, I made this one," he said. As she snickered, he added, "What? I got skills!"

They laughed and toasted each other with the sandwich halves.

"I wanted to talk about Stone Mountain," he said with a sly smile.

Lucy felt her breath leave her as the memory of their connection flooded her mind.

"I don't think there's anyone here that can't tell that I like you, Lucy. I like you a lot," he told her as he took her hand. "I came here looking for something, and now I believe I've found it, in you."

"I like you too, Micah, but there is something you need to know about..."

Micah cut her off, placing a finger on her lips. "You just told me everything I need to know." He wrapped his hand around the back of her neck and pulled her to him, into the kiss they both had been think- ing about since Georgia. She opened her eyes to see him smiling. "I had to do that before we head out. Jaso found something in the Language Arts Wing. I'll be waiting with the others at the ship when you're ready." Micah picked up the rest of his sandwich, and walked out the door.

Lucy tried to speak, but she seemed to have lost her voice. She touched her lips as her fingers were still quivering. "I'll... be right up?"

she said even though he had been gone for a good five minutes. She composed herself and grabbed her bag before heading to the Silvertooth. Lucy was walking through Gallery 305 toward the elevator when Walter approached her.

"Miss Ducit, if I may borrow a moment of your time, please."

"Make it fast, Walter. I have to meet the others," she said.

The odd little bot produced a small, folded piece of paper. "I found this laying on the floor outside the workshop. My optical scanners believe this to be the writing of Mr. Otto."

Lucy took the paper. It was a page from the diary that had been ripped out. She immediately dropped her backpack and searched for the diary. Scanning the pages, she found where it came from. "Someone took pages from the diary!" She ran for the elevator in a rush to speak with Stan. "Thank you, Walter!" she called over her shoulder.

Lucy reached the roof and saw James and Stan going over a supply list.

"We've got trouble, guys!" she shouted. She came to a sliding stop in front of them.

"Whoa! Calm down, kiddo. What's the problem?" asked Stan.

Lucy held the page out for them to see. "This is a page from Gramps's diary that was ripped out. I have always had the diary either on me or in my room . So, it's one of us... Who would tear pages out and why?" she asked.

James took the paper and looked it over. "Do you know what this section talked about? Have you read it?" he asked.

Lucy shrugged her shoulders. "Not sure. It's from the back, and I haven't gotten that far." She took the journal and flipped to the back where the pages came from. "It was the last entry, *'15 January, 2058; I don't know how long I can hide Lucy from the Countess now, my cover has been blown. I know they will be coming for me and when they do, they will find her. I'm too old to fight, and my machines are not as efficient as they once were. I have finally found the riddle Dadeag told me all those years ago. I need to get the information to Gerard and the others in case some-thing happens to me. The eyes of Lee are Gateway Stones. Where they lead, I'm still foggy on that. I think I went to find out, but my mind goes blank, almost like it was erased. The most disturbing thing I found out was that the Countess has a...'* The page ended." she read aloud to them.

Tears stained Lucy's face. She looked to Stan and James to try to make sense of things, "This is just days before he died. Do you think the Countess killed him for this? He wrote that she found out who he was and would be after him."

"I don't think that's what happened, dear," Stan said. "What concerns me more is the last line. The Countess has a what?"

James asked, "What does the torn-out page say?"

Lucy handed it to Stan who unfolded it and began to read aloud. "'This is not an official entry, I know, but I have figured out the keys! It was right in front of us this whole time. The priests that were present at the resurrection of Lazarus are not the keys. Azrael placed a curse on Caiaphas and his family, the five brothers of Ananus. I need to get this back to the Synod, but I must be careful. I know I'm being watched closely. Hopefully, with me staying on the run, it won't lead back to Lucy. The first key is the key of knowledge, find it and it will reveal the others. I am placing this journal inside one of my Enigma Boxes and sending it to the Met with a trusted friend in a steamer cab. I hope it's not too late." Stan started to cry and slowly shook her head. "He should have just come to us. We could have protected him."

"That's not what he wanted. He tried to draw their attention away from you... and me," Lucy said with her head hung low. "That's why he sent the box here and stayed in the open. He came to me the week he died, and it felt like he was saying good-bye forever, but I just thought he was going on some trip. Gramps was always going to differ-ent places." Lucy stopped and could see the last puzzle piece fall into place. "He didn't travel for fun, did he? It was always for the Synod." She searched their faces waiting for an answer. "Wasn't it?" Tears burned her eyes as she clenched her hands into fists. "He gave his life to protect you and this group. We better make damn sure we get that key before the Countess does." She placed her hands on her grandfather's pistols that were now strapped to her thighs in their holsters. "And if I find out that the pages were torn out by a traitor in this group, I will personally kill them."

Stan and James watched in silence as Lucy stormed up the ramp and onto the ship.

Micah and Jaso arrived in time to hear the shouts and see Lucy exit. "Everything okay?" Micah asked.

"Yes," Stan told him. "We will explain later. Did you guys find out anything about this long mountain?"

"We think we know where it is. In the 1800's Colorado was home to the Arapaho tribe. We believe that was their language, the language the stones were using at first," Jaso told them. "We found some mentions of the long mountain in the museum scrolls."

Micah added, "We did some cross-referencing, comparing old and new maps, and we believe we know what mountain the stones were talking about."

"Well, do you want us to guess?" James said holding his arms up and tapping his watch.

"It's Pike's Peak," Jaso said. "And that's not all. According to the archives, almost exactly two hundred years ago Julia Holmes became the first woman to climb to the top of Pike's Peak. This cannot be a coincidence."

Stan's brow furrowed. "Do we think this Julia Holmes was a Reaper?"

"It sounds like it to me, but can't be sure," Jaso answered. "We will go further in detail on board."

"This is starting to sound crazy, guys," Micah added. "Wait until you see the paperwork."

13 Julia Holmes

Jaso was convinced Julia Holmes was the last chosen that the stones spoke of.

"We don't know what we are going to face on that mountain-top. What I do know is that we must reach it before the Countess does," Jaso said.

"Yeah, that's what that scene was that you just saw. Lucy found some of the pages from Conrad's journal had been ripped out," Stan told them. "So Ruina may have someone on the inside, some kind of mole."

"That can't be possible, can it?" Jaso asked.

Stan shrugged her shoulders. "I hope not. I feel sorry for them if Lucy finds them if it is."

James looked at the materials and maps brought up by Micah and Jaso. "So, do we think this Julia Holmes was a Reaper? I mean, am I the only one that finds it odd that we are taking Lucy up almost exactly two hundred years from then?"

Micah flipped through some papers. "Here is something I found. It's a letter Julia wrote to her mother from the top of the mountain." He pushed the paper to the center of the table for all to see. "If you just read the words, it's just sentiment to her mother. Now, if you look harder, I believe she is telling her what actually happened."

Jaso read the letter read aloud,

"*Aug, 5th, 1858.*

Nearly everyone tried to discourage me from attempting it, but I believed that I should succeed; and now here I am. I feel that I would not have missed this glorious sight for anything at all."

James had a very confused look on his face. You could almost see his brain working with his eyes squinted, and head tilted to one side. "That says nothing about the key," he said. "What she did or had to do or anything. Am I missing something?" he asked.

Jaso laughed and took a small bottle of nitrous air from his pouch. "The first Reapers were not stupid. They had some pretty cool tricks up their sleeve. She wrote this on the top of Pike's Peak, where it's cold." He sprayed a light dusting of the frigid air across the letter. Soon, other lines and symbols appeared. "They couldn't risk just anyone reading this," he said with a wink.

They examined the letter once more,

"Nearly everyone tried to discourage me from facing the challenge of the first key, from attempting it, but I believed that I should succeed and end this torment at the hands of Satan's Captain; and here I am, by the grace of God, that I would not have missed this glorious battle and sight for anything at all."

Stan read this new version out loud then placed the letter back on the table. "She mentions Satan's Captain, could that be Ruina? I know she's immortal, but we have no records of her or her minions before she took office."

"Communications and records were not reliable then," James said. "The Countess could have been learning her power and it was passed off as folklore." He tapped his forehead with his finger trying to recall a story. "I remember hearing about a novel written in the late seventeen hundreds called *The Tale of the Black Forest.* It spoke of necromancy. It could have been her."

Jaso started to pace back and forth, rubbing the stubble on his chin, "Okay, this Julia Holmes went to find the first key. The Key of Knowledge. So, what happened? What went wrong? What happened to her after the climb?"

Micah shuffled the papers, "Hmm. There's nothing much about her after that. Her timeline just skips forward and speaks about her work with the National Women's Suffrage Movement, the New York Herald Tribune, and the Bureau of Education in Washington D.C. It's like it was a nice mountain hike and that's it."

Tapping her fingers on the table, Stan asked, "Why does the letter end that way? She mentions the battle but nothing afterward."

"I think she wrote this before the battle," Micah chimed in. "The question is what happened afterward? If she lost the battle, or whatever it was she engaged in, why did she not write it down for future reference?"

"It's almost as if her time as a Reaper was erased from that point forward," Jaso said to them.

"Well, we can't let that discourage us," Stan said. "We have to finish what she started."

They hear a loud boom as Lucy throws a cannister piston cleaner against a wall.

"We need to get this ship in the air before Lucy blows a gyro gasket up there," James told them. "She seemed pretty mad."

They gathered everything they thought would be needed and boarded the Silvertooth. Fire blazed in the furnaces and the balloon filled; they were soon airborne. It was nearly 1700 miles from the Met in New York to Pike's Peak in Colorado. A long journey was ahead of them, and they needed to be ready. Jaso paced back and forth across the deck. "We have a while before we get to the mountain, everyone needs to get some rest to be ready."

James set the ship to autopilot and everyone headed to their rooms, leaving just Stan and Jaso. James looked to Jaso. "I'll be back in few minutes to take watch. I won't be far, I just don't like my ship to fly without me."

Jaso gave him a nod and watched him descend into the cabin area.

"Jaso, sweetie, since we have some time do you want to talk?" she asked him. "I'd be more than happy to listen."

"There's nothing to talk about. I suggest we stay focused on the mission," he insisted.

"Well, just know that anytime you feel you're ready, I'll be here for you," Stan replied. She watched him walk away and disappear into the shadows of the hallway where the galley was located. She wiped a tear from her cheek, "One day. And when that day comes, I'll be ready."

They had been flying for what seemed to be forever when a whistle could be heard throughout the ship, followed by James's voice. "Pike's Peak straight ahead! Everyone needs to be top-side!"

The large, looming mountain-top was slowly coming into view. Snow covered peaks stretched upward, trying to reach heaven itself. The Silvertooth made its way toward the peak. "It's too quiet," Stan said. "I was expecting the Countess's foot soldiers."

Lucy shrugged her shoulders, "Maybe we beat them here. If we hurry, we might be gone before they even arrive."

"No, they're close," James said. "I can smell the stink of death."

"Do we even know where to go or what to do?" asked Micah.

"We need to have Lucy on the top of the peak when the moon reaches its highest," Stan said. "That is when the stones said she would see all." Stan curled her finger making air quotes when she said that.

James looked to the sky and checked his compass. "Well, that gives us about three hours to reach the top, get set up, and be ready for whatever we have coming our way. I'm ready to get this done and get back home. I hate the cold air."

"Why are we making a camp if we are trying to hurry?" Lucy asked.

"It's better to be prepared rather than caught by surprise in haste," James told her.

"Wow, that was pretty insightful, James," Micah said with eyes widened. He wasn't used to hearing that kind of motivation coming from the head tinker.

James just shifted his eyes. "That's what Conrad always told me."

The ship touched down on the snow-covered mountain as close to the top as they could get. There wasn't much room for the ship on the peak, but they found a flat area surrounded by beautiful red rock formations. The group filed out down the ramp. The ground crunched under Lucy's boots, uncovering a sign that read 'Pikes Peak Summit House'. She shivered in the chill of the night.

Micah came up behind her and placed his arms around her. "A little colder here than we expected."

"I don't feel the cold; I feel something else. I'm not sure what just yet."

"I estimate it will take an hour and a half to reach the peak," Jaso told them. "That will give us plenty of time to set up and prepare... for whatever."

As the moon rose in the night sky, the stars seemed brighter than ever before. The crisp coolness in the air whipped around them, mocking them, as if it knew they were outsiders. How long had it been since man set foot on these ridges? How many families made the trek and stood proudly together in this place posing for pictures before the Countess seemed to make the world crumble?

"It looks like I could pluck one of them from the sky and put it in my pocket," Lucy said reaching upward to the stars.

Micah laughed, "We are high on this peak, but not high enough for that."

Lucy punched him in the arm, "I'm not that dumb!" She furrowed her brow and hung her head. "I'm scared of what will happen. What if I'm not one of these chosen? What if I get the key, but something goes wrong? What if I can't get it? What if... "

Micah placed his finger to her lips, "Too many questions for right now. Though, I do have one for you." Lucy felt a lump form in her throat. She tried her best to speak, but the lump was about to suffocate her, so she just gave a nod of her head. He looked deep into her eyes. He could see the moon reflecting in them. "Do you have my six?"

She threw her arms around his neck and kissed him as if it were just them. No mountain, group or key. Just a boy and a girl. The kiss ended, and she opened her eyes to see him smiling. "So, does that mean yes?" Lucy gave him a shove.

"It's time, everyone," Jaso called to the group. "Let's be ready for anything. This will be base camp. Leave no stone unturned."

14 Pike's Peak

Micah helped Lucy with her gear while everyone was setting up tents, tables, and gadgets to help prepare for what might be coming. With so little to go on, they didn't know what to expect. You could feel the nervous excitement throughout the group. This is the closest they had ever been to any of the keys.

"You ready?" Micah asked her as he tightened the straps on her gun belt.

"Surprisingly, yes," she answered. "I'm confident we can handle whatever comes. We got this!"

He smiled, "You got my six?"

"Always, because I know you have mine," she replied. "Why do you keep asking me that?"

He flashed a smile. "Because I like hearing you say it."

The hike to the top of Pike's Peak wasn't as hard on the group of Reapers as it was on Julia Holmes two hundred years ago. She had to climb uncharted trails and mountain ledges, clawing her way to the top. Now, there was a path cleared to the top that was used by tourists in the early 1900s. People could drive their motorcars all the way to the top if they wanted. The path was cluttered with trees and huge rocks that had fallen over the years, but it was still easy enough. They walked in silence, keeping their eyes peeled for any sign of the Countess or her soldiers.

Lucy was blowing heat rings in the chilly night air with her breath. "Looks like someone isn't nervous at all. Eh, kiddo?" Stan asked.

"No, I'm nervous, but confident at the same time," she answered. "That's what I was telling Micah. I have a good feeling about this." She flashed a smile and patted her backpack where the journal was. "I have to be confident and careful. If I fail to do what I need to do, then Gramps died in vain. I can't live with that."

Stan put her arm around Lucy's shoulders, "You sure you're only nineteen? You sound like someone with everything in order."

"I'll be twenty next month!"

"Well now," Stan said. "That makes a world of difference!"

They laughed and followed in behind the rest of the group. They all walked about thirty minutes more before James announced, "Welcome to Pikes Peak, everyone."

Jaso looked up at the night sky. The clouds were rolling away as if they knew their part as well. "The moon should be reaching its highest point at any moment. Everyone ready?" he asked. "If things start to go sideways fall back to the camp. We don't want to face the Countess on this peak."

Lucy took a deep breath, feeling the crisp air burn her lungs, and gave a nod to Jaso. She found a cleared area that seemed to overlook the world as it slept. "This is amazing. I never knew the world could be this silent, this beautiful," said Lucy. "Now I know why Julia Holmes called it a glorious sight."

Jaso directed the others to form a circle around Lucy, "Hold your positions and watch for anything. We don't want to be caught by surprise."

Moonlight bathed the ground in a pale, eerie glow all around her. The last of the clouds rolled away to reveal the moon; it was so bright it was almost as if it was daybreak. The silence was loud enough it caught Lucy off guard. The air seemed to shimmer like heat waves rising from hot pavement.

"This can't be good," Lucy said to herself. "Brace yourself, Lucy."

As her eyes began to refocus, she could see a man standing in front of her. He was dressed in translucent robes that flowed around him, even without the wind blowing. She looked to his face, gentle eyes of blue stared directly at her from behind loose strands of hair tied up inside a turban.

"Oh, my God!" she gasped. The man's mouth had been sewn shut. "Guys, are you seeing this?" No answers came. "Stan? Micah?" she said, slowly turning to look behind her. All of them were frozen in time. Standing like statues in a museum ready for display.

"Your friends will be of no service to you this night." The voice came from James but it wasn't his own. "Their fates hinge on you, chosen one." This time the same voice came from Stan's body.

Lucy pulled both pistols from their holsters and pointed them directly at the man. "Who are you?" she demanded. "Are you one of the Countess's new toys? What have you done to them?"

"They are perfectly all right, for the time being," the voice boomed from Micah. "Your weapons are not needed. You are your own weapon now."

"For the time being? What does that mean?" Lucy asked.

Jaso's body spoke up, "You are of the chosen, and they are not. Their future now depends on you."

"No! This is between us and only involves us!" she shouted. "If I lose, you let them live." She could feel herself start to tremble. The guns in her hands shook so hard she had to tighten her grip to keep from dropping them.

The spirit came closer, and the guns seemed to pass through him. "I will not harm them, that is not in my power. If you fail your trial, you will forfeit your existence and your claim to the keys. All memory of this encounter, your trial, your friends, will all fade and be erased from their minds and yours," the voice came this time from the spirit itself. "If you succeed, I grant you the first key, and you grant me my needed release."

"Why not just give me the key," Lucy suggested. "That way we are both happy."

"Because he will know. He is everywhere, and nowhere. It is by his will we suffer our torment. All key holders must obey his commands," the voice said. "We must suffer for our actions against The Angel of Death. We must be death, and death is fair to everyone. No one, no matter place or creed can escape the sting of Azrael."

"No one except the Countess, that is," she said with her voice trembling. "I have to stop her."

"The one you speak of will also taste the sting. Whether by you or another, it is foretold. We are the ones that helped create the monster you call the Countess, and if you can pass the trials you will return her to mortality," the spirit told her.

Feeling her nerves start to settle Lucy lowered her pistols and returned them to her holsters. "Let's do this thing then. What do I have to do?"

15 Trial of the Key

The spirit lifted his arms and time slowed to a stop. Lucy found herself surrounded by blank, nothingness.

"My name is Ananus, first priest of my order. I am the holder of the Key of Knowledge. Your task is simple, yet great. Tedious to the mind, and joyous to the soul. Do you accept your challenge and all of its warnings?" he asked.

Lucy stiffened her body in a battle stance. "I accept your challenge," she said with a nod.

Thunder boomed in the distance as the spirit drifted closer to her. "Then it begins."

The priest placed his left hand behind her head looking straight into her eyes. The cool blue color she saw before had faded to a black that resembled a pool of tar. She was scared but stayed steady. The spirit touched her forehead with his finger. Instantly, Lucy saw flashes of light that formed into pictures. Pictures that were memories from her past. People she knew, places she had been, things she had done.

"What is this?" she asked. "What does this have to do with the key?"

"Your life is your trial," the voice said. "Truth is the key. You must use truth to unlock falsehoods and doubt."

The images slowed down and focused on an instance showing a small girl. This girl, who looked to be around three or four years of age, was sitting alone and crying.

"Why does the girl cry?" he asked.

"I don't know," she answered.

A sharp pain pierced through her mind. Lucy shrieked out in pain grabbing her head, but remained upright.

"Lies will not serve you here. They will not benefit you or me. Look closer and tell me why the girl cries."

She opened her eyes and studied the image. Lucy knew this girl... it was her. It was Lucy as a child.

"She is crying because she is afraid," she said. "She's away from her parents and is scared of what might happen."

"Of what might happen to her?" the voice asked. "Remember, only truth will suffice."

A stern look formed on her face, "No."

"No? Afraid of what might happen to others?" he asked.

A tear trickled down from Lucy's right eye, "She's afraid of what will happen to her parents without her."

Ananus asked, "Where is the girl at?"

Lucy scanned the area around her. She saw the image as if she was there again, watching as a visitor.

"We were at the flower park in New Haven on a family holiday," she answered. "I went to look at this beautiful butterfly that I saw land on a sunflower. The butterfly flew away, and I turned back to my parents, but they were gone. I ran up and down the rows of flowers looking, searching for any sign of them."

In Lucy's vision she ran along with her younger self.

"Why did you fear for them and not yourself," he asked. "You were a child lost; your parents needed to save you, not for you to save them."

The spirit of Ananus seemed to be changing. His form was not as before. The robes were the same, but his face was now hidden behind a veil of mist.

"I needed to help them. I felt like I needed to, at least."

Again, the spirit stated, "You were a child, why did you feel they needed protection and not yourself?"

"I... don't... know," Lucy answered in an annoyed tone.

Again, the pain shot through her skull, buckling her knees this time. She screamed as she dropped to the ground.

"Unacceptable answer," he said. "The way to obtain the key is to fill the well of knowledge. Only truth can fill the well and set us free. True knowledge cannot be a lie. Your answers will save you or destroy you."

Lucy wiped her face with the back of her hand. Slowly getting to her feet, "I don't understand what this has to do with the key." She waited, and he offered no response. He stood perfectly still, silent and staring at her with his cold eyes piercing through the mist. "Ask your questions then."

"Why did you fear for your parents?" he asked again.

Lucy searched her memories, every emotion, and looked deep inside of the darkness she didn't even know existed inside her. Finally, she looked to Ananus, "I was stronger than them. I could feel something inside of me telling me I had to protect them. They needed me."

The form of Ananus shifted and phased, changing into an image that was too familiar to Lucy.

"Gramps? Is that you?" she asked as every fiber of her body began to shake.

A gentle smile graced the face of the old man. Lucy ran for him with her arms open, but he held up his hand to stop her.

"This is not Conrad Otto, though, I do remember him well. Your bloodline flows from him. He tried to acquire the key and would have succeeded if he had been of the chosen. I could not erase his entirety, so I took his memory of the key. He was a just and honorable man, and from him, your power grows. Trust in yourself and answer this: Why does the girl cry?"

She clenched her hands in frustration. Screaming in anger she charged the spirit who now wore the face of her grandfather. He held up his right hand and stopped her in her tracks.

"ARRRGHH!" she screamed in pain.

"Do not fight knowledge," he said. "You cannot hide the truth behind lies. Lies eventually fade and disappear, but truth is ever constant. Truth never changes."

"I saw them die!" Lucy exclaimed "I saw them leave me and I was afraid. I cried because I thought my dreams were coming true!" Lucy shouted as she dropped to her knees again, sobbing uncontrollably. "I was only four years old, but I knew. I knew what was coming and couldn't do anything to stop it! I was only four!"

Ananus knelt in front of her, "You have a gift so rare and special, you do not even realize it. Therefore, you were chosen." He took her hand, "Your parents did not die this day?"

Lucy looked up to see her grandfather's face again, "No. They came back to find me. They were so relieved and happy. But still, they died four years later."

"How did they perish?" he asked her.

"I was told it was an automobile accident."

"Was that how you saw their end?" he asked.

Lucy choked back her answer. "No... I didn't see it happen that way." She closed her eyes as memories flooded her mind. "In my dreams, I saw them burning. Trapped inside a building as the flames grew all around them. They held each other until the end."

The spirit was not moved, no emotion or cares. "Did you warn them of this?" he asked.

Lucy's brow furrowed in frustration. "I was just a kid! A kid with bad dreams. Who would believe that?" she exclaimed.

"Belief is not the responsibility of the one telling the story; it is that of the one's hearing the warning. Your gift is of the Daxeal, the chosen," he told her.

"My turn for a question," Lucy stated with her hands on her hips. "What exactly is this Daxeal?"

"The Daxeal are angels of the Roman church, direct adversaries of Azrael and his minions of death," he said. "They choose mortals to assist them in containing his cruelty and stay the course of his orders. If a chosen can pass the five trials of the priests, they will hold the power to unlock the cursed essence left behind in Lazarus and release us from our bonds."

Ananus presented a chain made of pure gold from around his neck. Attached to the chain was a single key of brass adorned with a golden dragonfly and the green gem of despair. It was the Key of Knowledge. This was the first step in stopping the Countess.

"Your trial is almost complete, chosen. If you answer truthfully and embrace the knowledge, you will release me and obtain the first key of Lazarus," he said. The spirit came closer to her, face to face locking eyes with her. He took her hands in his own, "If you fail to answer truthfully, you not only forfeit the opportunity to the key, you forfeit your life as you know it."

Lucy felt a lump form in her throat that seemed impossible to swallow. Her heart raced and pounded in her chest causing her breath to catch, but she summoned the courage to nod her head and squeak out the words through trembling lips, "I'm ready."

Once again, all sounds were silenced. All movement stopped in time. The cool mountain air was thick and heavy on her exposed skin; Lucy felt sweat starting to bead on her forehead despite the frigid air. She felt as though he could see her soul directly as she prepared for his question:

"Why did the girl cry?"

Lucy became furious. "I've answered that question already!" she shouted. "Were you not paying attention?"

She saw the eyes of Ananus turn black as a moonless night. His form shifted to that of a demon looking for vengeance. A ringing sound shot through her head; unbelievable pain forced tears down her face.

"I thought you might be the one to release me!" he shouted. "You are just like the others!" The form of Ananus shifted to that of fire. Burning bright without heat. Blinding light and pain coursing around Lucy. Fire was everywhere she looked.

Lucy began to panic, screaming as the pressure started to grow inside her, her mind growing cloudy. She clenched her fingers into her hair. "What do you want from me? I cried because I was a scared little girl!" she shouted at the top of her lungs. "I thought I was alone. My parents were gone, and I would never see them again. I cried... I cried because I didn't die with them!"

Suddenly, the pain stopped, and Lucy looked to the spirit standing in front of her. He had returned to his original form. His head tilted upwards as his eyes fixed on the heavens.

"Your mouth... the laces are untying," she said.

The laces sewn into the mouth of Ananus were unraveled and freeing his voice. "Please, go on," he said in his own voice for the first time in hundreds of years. His eyes full of compassion and wonderment now.

Lucy's shoulders slumped as she lowered her head. Tears flowed freely from her eyes down her cheeks; she felt more vulnerable than she ever had before.

"My worst fear in life is to wind up alone. Like I am now. My dreams were so real I could feel their pain as they died and mine as they left me," she wiped her face with her hands and continued. "When I couldn't find them, my mind began to race; I couldn't breathe. I felt utterly alone."

"Your parents did die, later, and you were not alone. The Daxeal showed you your future, the fate of your parents, to prepare you, to ready you for your fear. This is the power of knowledge," he told her. "And you found yourself not alone."

"No, I wasn't alone. My grandfather came and took care of me. Now that I think about it, seeing them die over and over did seem to ease the shock when it happened. I know that sounds odd, but it's true," Lucy said with a smile. "I was told it was an automobile accident and that I was actually with them."

Ananus said, "You knew that to be an untruth. Knowledge does not stand on untruths and falsehoods. You had seen them perish and you were there when it happened, but not in the automobile. The knowledge will fill you and you will have sight beyond seeing."

"Why would the Reapers lie to me?" she asked. "Even now, as I found out the secret of what Gramps did to save me; they still say it was a car accident."

"They do not have the knowledge of truth. Their eyes are still clouded by the untruth of your grandfather," he told her.

"Gramps kept all this a secret from everyone... why?" she pondered.

Ananus smiled, and held out his hand. "That is a lesson of love. A lesson you will soon learn."

Lucy stood upright and took the spirits' hand. "I chose to believe it. I chose to be just a kid that lost her parents. Now, I choose to be the woman that avenges them for their injustice." Fire burned inside her, the essence of the Daxeal could be felt as she stood for the first time as a chosen. "I have answered your question, I have given you the truth. Where is the key?"

16 The Truth Shall Set You Free

A smile grew on the face of Ananus. Lucy gasped in shock, but relief could be seen in the ancient priest's face. They both looked down to see the blade of a sickle protruding from his chest.

"Thank you, Lucy Ducit, chosen one of the Daxeal. You are the one we have waited for," Ananus said as his form began to vanish.

Standing in his place was a tall, hooded figure with bone fingers wrapped around the handle of a long-bladed sickle. His other hand pulled the hood from his face to reveal the face of death and darkness, Azrael himself.

Lucy was surprised, to say the least. He was not this hideous, gross monstrosity hell bent on collecting souls, but an extremely attractive male with blond hair and soft gray eyes. She gasped at seeing his true, luscious form.

"You have released the priest Ananus from his bonds." His voice was that of an angel singing early in the morning to raise the morning sun, almost melodic. "The Daxeal has chosen wisely with you. Claim your prize as I have finally claimed one of mine. Release the soul of Lazarus and reap the essence of wickedness from this world." Azrael lowered the blade of his sickle to Lucy. Hanging from the blade was the key of knowledge. "Knowledge is the key that unlocks many doors. Use it wisely," he told her.

Lucy reached out her hand and took hold of the key. As her fingers wrapped around it, visions flashed before her mind's eye: places, people, spirits, and even her grandfather. Lucy was transported before a bright light overlooking fields of golden sunflowers. Standing beside the light was Azrael dressed in brightly colored robes of blues and white, not his black robes of reaping.

"You were once my prize, Lucy," Azrael told her. "That is until Conrad Otto breathed life back into you. One day you will be mine again. You have seen with your own eyes; no one escapes death. Everyone pays the price."

He disappeared leaving only Lucy standing before the light. His voice rang out inside her mind, "You have done well, child of the Daxeal. Use the knowledge given you to fulfill your birth rite. You were given these gifts for a purpose, and your gifts will serve you well. Stay the course, and free the others."

The voice faded. The visions left her weak and overloaded with thoughts not her own. She felt her knees buckling under her. Arms stretching, grasping for anything to steady her, she hit the ground. She was back on Pikes Peak surrounded by her friends.

"Where did he go?" shouted Jaso. "He just vanished."

Stan rushed to Lucy. "Lucy! Oh no, Lucy! Are you alright, kiddo?"

Micah came to a skidding stop, dropping the Sentai blades at his side. He placed a hand under her head and tilted her forward. "Lucy, you still with us?" he asked as his eyes filled with concern.

Her eyes slowly started to drift open, "Why wouldn't I be?" she said faintly. "We're a team. I need to have your six." A rush of relief filled the them. A collective sigh of relief could be heard from everyone.

Lucy sat up, rubbing her head, "And I have this." She opened her hand to reveal a key, the Key of Knowledge.

"Oh, my God. She did it," James shouted. "She actually got the first key!"

"Congratulations, Miss Ducit. You are the first person to claim a key after all this time."

The group snapped their heads around to see a woman standing on the ridge with her hands placed on her hips. She was dressed in a black dress with a tight corset trimmed in red. She wore a hat that looked early Victorian with a thin black lace veil covering her face. She looked like she stepped out of one of the paintings in the Met. Standing on either side of her were rather large humanoid figures scarred from head to toe, like one of Frankenstein's monsters. Each one had a smaller creature strapped to its back, holding reins to control them. The reins were attached to the side of the abomination's head by a bolt that ran through it. On their chests they bore the symbol of the Countess; infinity on fire.

"You know who I am, and you know you cannot defeat me," she said with arms stretched outward in a revealing motion. "Let's just save a lot of bloodshed, yours exclusively, and time by just handing that key over now. I promise to kill you quickly without pain... well, not much," the Countess told them.

Jaso pulled his rifles, "Stan, get Lucy out of here. We will hold them as long as we can." He turned back to the Countess. "We decline your offer, but there is something we can give you."

Ruina placed her hands on her hips again and gave a condescending smile, "What would that be, little Reaper?"

A low humming whistle was heard in the distance. It came louder and louder until something hit the abomination on her left with a thud, knocking him off-balance. The little creature on its back tried to dismount frantically.

"We will give you hell!" shouted Jaso, as the projectile lodged in the chest of the beast exploded.

The blast was so strong it knocked the Countess to the ground. Flat on her back, her ears ringing from the blast, she shouted, "Kill them! Kill them all and bring me that key!"

A horde of minions charged forward from behind her, and the hulking blob that was left slowly lumbered toward them. The little creature driving started screeching orders, hopping up and down on its back. James opened fire with both cannons dropping soldier after soldier, waiting for the Delta Charge to be ready again.

The remaining abomination reached James and unleashed a mammoth blast on the mini tank sending it flying backwards. It took out three of the Davarti just from the sheer motion.

Micah found himself surrounded by four of the undead soldiers. He grasped the handles of the Sentai blades and placed them in front of him. The right blade he held horizontal as the left was held steady above his head. One of the Davarti fired a blast from his side gun, Micah quickly shifted the blades and deflected the bullets back, jamming the gun and causing a chain reaction inside the chambers; the gun exploded in the hands of the Davarti. He spun to his left scything the blades across the neck of another, separating its head from its body. The two remaining soldiers charged together; electrified weapons lit the air, with sparks flying in every direction.

Micah stepped back into a battle stance, calm and stoic. At the last moment, he crouched low, swords swinging to each side. The blades severed the legs of the oncoming soldiers just below the knees, sending them to the ground. With a boot to the chest and a blade to their throats, they were sent from this world. Free of assailants, Micah rushed to help Jaso.

Lucy started to shake the cobwebs from her head and noticed that she was being led away from the fight and her friends by Stan. She started to squirm trying to break Stan's grasp.

"Easy, kiddo. We don't know what went on inside you," Stan said as they came to a stop.

Lucy rubbed her head and looked inside her clenched fist to see the key on its chain. "I did it, I really did it!" she exclaimed.

"I know," said Stan. "Unfortunately, so do they." Stan pointed to the fight waging behind them. Lucy could see the Countess standing in the center barking orders.

"We have to help them," Lucy yelled. "There are too many of them. They'll all die!"

Stan stood in front of her with her arms outstretched to stop her. "Our priority is to get you and that key to safety. We all are willing to lay our life on the line for that key. They won't be able to buy us much time so we have to hurry."

Lucy felt her blood boil as she looked at the Countess. Memories from the trial flooded her mind; how the countess had taken all her family. Her face ran red with anger. She could see her friends being slowly overrun by the minions.

"I'm not leaving them. I have seen my fate, and it's not here, not today." Lucy pulled the chain around her neck and shoved the key inside her shirt. "I'm sure I will need help in a few seconds... if you don't mind," she told Stan.

"What are you..."

"Hey! Ruina! You want the key? I'm right here," Lucy shouted as she pulled the Rainmakers from her holsters. "Come get it."

"Get me that infuriating girl and get me that key!" the Countess shrieked. "Try to keep her alive. If not, so be it!"

The soldiers stopped and turned their attention on Lucy. The creature riding the last behemoth ordered it to stop pounding on James and the mini tank and go for the key.

Blast after blast, Lucy downed Davarti. Firing shot after shot and reloading with little effort. Suddenly, the loud whistling sound was heard again. The little creature driving the abomination started to panic.

"Much boom! Much boom!" it screeched as it pulled back on the reins trying to get the creature to stop. With a thud, the shell lodged in the chest of the behemoth, and the driver jumped off. Lucy dropped to the ground, covering her head as the Delta charge exploded and scattered undead parts all over the ground again. Some of the Davarti were missing their legs, others their arms, but still they tried to get to Lucy.

"Did ya miss us?" asked James as he came rolling into sight.

Micah came running from behind him followed by Jaso. They stood with Lucy and Stan ready to finish the fight.

"Are you scared to fight your own battles, Ruina?" shouted Jaso. "It seems we broke all of your toys," he said as he fired a shot into the Davarti torso that was crawling toward them.

They could see the red of her face behind her black lace veil. "My name... Is... THE COUNTESS!" she shouted. The remaining Davarti, swarmed in around their master. "I will have the key. I will harness its power, as I did from Lazarus, and I will become a god!" Ruina's eyes turned as black as smoke from a coal foundry. Shadows oozed from deep inside her.

"Don't let her touch your skin," Stan told Lucy. "She will drain the life from you and make you like a soldier."

Jaso opened fire on the approaching foot soldiers. The Countess grabbed two of the soldiers, one in each hand with surprising ease. She hoisted them up in front of her and used them as shields from the on-coming spray of gunfire. The shadows floated from the Countess to the bullet-filled Davarti, weaving in and out of the bullet holes like a tamed cobra.

"You cannot win," she told them. "The keys are a part of MY destiny."

She hurled the lifeless bodies toward the heroes. As they hit the frozen ground, the bodies turned to shadow vipers. James rolled his chair past them all to the front and shifted into the mini arsenal.

"I hate snakes!" he yelled, as he unleashed thousands of hot ammo rounds onto the slithering snakes.

Micah, Stan, and Jaso rushed to cover Lucy. Lucy patted her chest, wincing in pain. "What is burning?" she shouted as she pulled the key from her shirt. "The gem inside the key is glowing hot," she said to Micah.

"What is it doing?" asked Micah. "Is it a trick?"

Lucy squinted her eyes and held the key tightly in her grasp. Just like before, she saw images and heard sounds that pierced her mind. "I understand," she said dropping the key back into her shirt. Lucy placed her pistols back in their holsters and slowly walked around her friends and headed straight for the Countess.

"Lucy! What are you doing?" shouted Stan. "You need to stay behind us, hun!"

The Davarti saw her and charged in her direction. One by one, she ripped them to shreds with her bare hands using techniques that were not taught to her.

"Where did she learn that?" asked Micah, with his mouth agape.

Stan shrugged her shoulders. "Certainly not from me."

"WELL, SHOULDN'T WE be helping her instead of just watching?" Jaso exclaimed. "We'll have to ask her later."

The group ran to back her up, and they could hear her chanting ancient words that no one understood. Her face was blank and stone cold. Her eyes fixed on the Countess.

"Sha'nay eletor concurum. Sha'nay eletor concurum," Lucy repeated over and over as she made her way toward the Countess.

"Yes, child. You will make a grand addition to my Davarti."

"What is she doing?" asked James. "The Countess will drain her, take the key, and damn us all!"

"We have to stop her one way or another," said Jaso. "We can't let the Countess get the key." Jaso pulled his rifle and had Lucy in his sight. "Lucy! Please stop!" he shouted.

Stan felt her heart crash. "Cover me; I'll get her." The elder Reaper ran directly in front of Jaso, blocking his shot on Lucy. Stan was remarkably in shape for her age, but the battle was catching up to her. "Come on!" she said as she placed her hands on her hips, forcing air into her lungs. Pushing forward through the pain, she got close to Lucy. "You can't fight her hand to hand; you can't fight her at all while she has the Lazarus Gem. She feeds on the essence of the living, you have to stop!"

Lucy did stop. Turning to face Stan with an eerie, blank look that startled her. Stan felt a lump form in her throat as Lucy spoke.

"I am death eternal. I am the life of the undead. I am Azrael, and I claim these souls!"

The words came from Lucy but were from The Angel of Death himself. The Countess lunged for the girl, grasping for her throat, knocking an unsuspecting Stan back. Lucy's hands moved with perfection in motion blocking every move. With her left hand, she pushed Ruina off balance as she connected with her right fist just below the Countess's left eye. In one fluid motion, she left the ground, planting her knees in Ruina's chest, driving her to the ground with a thud to her back. The blow to her eye had opened her skin, and a single drop of blood oozed out. It had been hundreds of years since Ruina had felt pain. For the first time since she absorbed the Lazarus Gem, she was afraid. In a move of desperation, she grabbed the bare skin of Lucy's forearms.

"Now, you and the first key will be mine!"

17 Shock and Awe

Fear spread across the faces of the Reapers looking on in horror. They could see all hope fading. Ruina was turning Lucy and would take the key.

"Get away from her! Get her hands off!" shouted Stan as she tried to get up. "Lucy, please! Fight her!" The cold ground had opened a deep gash in the palm of her hand, but she didn't even notice. Her focus was on Lucy.

Jaso ran toward them, hoping to separate them before Ruina drained all the life from Lucy.

Micah was not far behind, blades in hand slicing at anything that moved. The Countess had her fingernails deep into the skin of Lucy. Her laugh had a maniacal tone dripping with confidence. Suddenly a deafening scream could be heard that had everyone stopping, even the Davarti, in their tracks. All eyes fell to Lucy and the Countess. The smirk had faded from Ruina's face as she stared at Lucy's cold blank expression. The scream had come from the Countess, not Lucy. Pain. The Countess felt pain.

"What are you doing?" the Countess shouted. "This is not possible!" She felt her hands burning. "You... you can't be!" she shouted in utter disbelief. "Arrgghh!" She let go of Lucy's arms and tried to kick her way out from underneath her. She quickly rose to her feet and looked down at Lucy who was still on her hands and knees, "What are you?"

In a low tone, like a reverb from a baritone, Lucy answered without looking up. "I am fear. I am judgment. I am YOUR judgment."

Frozen in shock, the Countess called for a retreat, "Retreat! We fight another day! Back to the ship!" She stopped and locked eyes with Lucy who was now standing, still trying to process what had just happened and looking down to her hands. The red, glistening blisters began to fade. "We will meet again, dear, and next time, I will be ready!" she shouted.

Micah had made his way behind the Countess. As she turned to flee, Micah swung with all his might barely missing her with the deadly Sentai blade. He did connect the handle of his weapon with little effect. The Countess grabbed him by the chest harness and threw him into Lucy, who was walking toward her, knocking them both to the ground. This gave Ruina enough time to reach her airship with the Synod looking on.

"I will be ready next time, little Reaper. I will have your head and that key as my trophy. You cannot meddle with my destiny!" Ruina shouted from the side rails of her airship.

On the ground, everyone had gathered around Lucy who remained lying flat on her back as she rubbed her head.

"Oh, my head... what hit me?" she said.

"That would be Micah," James said with a chuckle.

Micah sat up placing both hands on his head trying to keep it from swirling. "Not funny, James," he said. "I was just barrel rolled by an elderly woman."

Stan laughed and said, "It happens sometimes."

Jaso knelt on one knee. "I'm glad to see you're all right, Lucy," he said placing a hand on her shoulder. "Please tell me you still have the key."

Lucy frantically patted her shirt, feeling for the key around her neck. Grasping the chain, she pulled it from beneath her undershirt. "Whew! Yes, sir, I do," she said with a smile. She held it out for the group to see it.

Stan started to cry. "I can't believe it. We actually have the first key of Lazarus and sent the Countess running in defeat." She buried her face in the palms of her hands, "Oh I wish Conrad and Gerard could have been here."

"Maybe this news will help Gerard get better quicker," Lucy told her.

"Yes, let's head back to the ship. He worked his entire life for this; he needs to be a part of it," Jaso said.

"Yeah, I'm starting to not like these mountains," James told them. The team all looked in his direction. "Well, I never liked them, but now I like them even less."

THEY LOADED UP ON THE Silvertooth and headed back to New York. The group didn't say much, just did their parts to get the ship back in the air. As James set the autopilot they all went their separate ways trying to process what they had witnessed. Lucy was in her cabin tracing the details of the key with her finger when a knock at her door brought her back to reality. She placed the key inside the back pouch of Conrad's diary, placed it inside her backpack and tossed it into a chair.

"Come in, it's open," she said.

The door opened to reveal Micah holding two glasses and a bottle of sparkling apple water. "Care to celebrate with me?" he asked. He sat on the side of the bed next to Lucy and handed her a glass. "I saw that this was your favorite, so I stashed a bottle on here... just in case."

Lucy held her glass as he filled it about halfway. Micah raised his glass, "A toast."

"A toast to what?"

"What do you mean, 'to what?' Our first successful mission together. To finding the first key... and to finding us," he told her.

Lucy's cheeks began to flush a bright shade of pink. "To us?" she asked as she took a long sip from her glass trying to hide her smile. The bubbles tickled her nose, and she giggled. She never took her eyes from his.

"Yes, us," he said. "I can't hide how I feel about you. I don't even want to try and hide it." He took Lucy's glass from her and set both glasses down on the table. Then he took her hands in his and looked into her eyes. "And it seems you feel the same? At least, I'm hoping you do."

Lucy bit her bottom lip to hide her excitement. She thought she would scream at any moment, but that would ruin the moment, and she definitely did not want this moment to stop.

"When we were on that mountain peak, all I could think about was keeping you safe," Micah said. "Not the key, not the mission, just you. I promised you that I would have your back..."

Lucy placed her finger this time on his lips and leaned in close to him. "You did have my back," she said softly in his ear. "And now I want you to have all of me." She placed her hand behind his head and pulled him to her, and their bodies tangled together with him above her. "I will always have your six," Lucy said.

18 A Warrior Falls

As they touched down on the roof of the Met in New York, Jaso's voice rang out through the ship.

"Great job, everyone. Get cleaned up and grab some rest. Let's meet back in the lounge in two hours."

Micah closed the door to Lucy's room behind him to see Stan looking back at him harshly.

"Did you? Did she? Why were you... "

Micah laughed a little and said, "Shhhh. See you in the lounge." He gave her a wink, and walked past her.

She watched as he walked out of the sleeping quarters. "Oh, I know that boy did not just shush me!" She shook her head and knocked on Lucy's door.

"Door's open, come in," Lucy said almost singing.

When Stan walked in, she saw Lucy smiling bigger than she had ever seen.

"First thing, be careful. I know I'm not your mother and I know you are an adult, but just be careful," Stan said glancing away. "Believe me, I know. Second thing, I am so proud of you. I wanted to talk, just us, before we all get together to debrief the mission. You are an extremely special person; Conrad would be so proud, I know I am." She leaned in and gave Lucy a tight hug, "See you in a bit, hun. You did good."

"Thank you, Stan. It really does make me feel better to actually have a purpose, to belong. I don't remember much about my mom, but what I do remember is how she loved me," Lucy said with a huge smile. "I am honored to have you stand in her absence."

Lucy sat there and watched Stan go through the door, closing it behind her. She grabbed the diary from her backpack and opened it to a random page. "What words of wisdom do you have for me today, Gramps?"

'23 December 1998; I have met so many good people here in New York. So many that are dedicated to proving that Ruina Baxter is not what she claims to be. We just need to find proof! My days have been filled with friendship. Gerard and Alyssa are great friends, and Emily is the cutest. I have longed to have what they have many times. Today, I have found the answer to my prayers. I don't even know her name... yet. She is so beautiful, so electric, so out of my league. Do I dare try to live a normal life? Do I bring someone else into this crazy world I'm in? I know as time goes on, and we fight against Ruina, things could get dangerous, and being a member of the Synod, it will be worse. I must talk to her. I need to at least tell her how I feel. What am I saying? She will think I'm a lunatic! For now, I will admire the gorgeous brunette with the piercing green eyes from afar. So, until I get the nerve, or next time, whichever comes first, good night.'

"I know how you felt, Gramps," Lucy said. She held the diary to her chest. "I'm glad you finally got the nerve to ask her out." She put the diary back into the backpack and headed to get a shower and a change of clothes. The cabins of the Silvertooth were great, but she wanted to be back in the Met in her own room deep inside Gallery 305. Lucy walked down the ramp to the rooftop and saw Jaso and Stan talking to the house bot Walter. Jaso placed his hands behind his head and leaned forward. Stan covered her face and ran inside weeping with Jaso close behind.

"Is everything all right, Walter?" she asked.

"I'm afraid not, Miss Ducit," Walter said. "It's Dr. Hamilton. I'm afraid his condition has taken a turn for the worse."

Lucy quickly ran for the med bays. Jaso and Stan were already at Gerard's bedside. He was awake, but barely hanging on to life. He motioned for Jaso to come closer, and the young Hamilton leaned down to his father; tears streamed down his face as Gerard whispered something in his ear.

"I understand, father," Jaso assured him. "We have the first key. We actually have the upper hand on the Countess this time. We will finish the work you started," Jaso told him, his body quivering and his voice shaky, as he struggled to stay strong.

"Wait. Why will we finish it?" Lucy exclaimed. "He will be there with us to help and finish this himself." Lucy pulled the diary from the backpack, and the key from the pouch, "We have the key! Gerard, look! We have the Key of Knowledge, and I can now find the others. We, as a team, will beat her."

Gerard strained to form a satisfied smile as he looked to Lucy.

"I am now complete. I leave you with the knowledge to make this world whole again," Gerard said to her. Turning to Stan, "You were the love that could have been. I am so sorry for not embracing you," he said as a single tear rolled down his face. "Take care of him."

Stan placed her hand on his cheeks trying not to shake too much, "You were always the one." She kissed him softly on the forehead, "It's okay if you want to go to them. Go find Alyssa and Emily; rest, my love, you deserve it."

"No, not yet!" Lucy exclaimed. "I have so many more questions."

Gerard closed his eyes and laid his head back on the pillow still holding on to Stan's hand. The air in the room became still and silent. Lucy saw Azrael once more come into the room, no one else could see him.

"Come, brave Reaper, your time is now," he said softly. "You fought long and hard. Your rewards await."

Stan and Jaso were still on either side of his bed, oblivious to the angel claiming his prize. Lucy watched as Gerard's spirit rose from his body. Not the elderly, broken body of the man she grew to love, but a younger self. Before her stood, a tall, muscular young man who reminded her of Jaso. Broad shoulders looming above her, wearing a black vest with silver buttons in the front. A black rimmed derby with his flight goggles on his forehead. The bright orange scarf around his neck was gently waving, even though there was no air moving.

He held out his hand, and a young ebony skinned girl with bouncy curls came running in and held tight to his arm. She was so young, so innocent, not much younger than Lucy. Behind her was a beautiful woman with caramel skin dressed in a gorgeous Victorian style, long dress coat with brass buttons running the length of the lapel all the way up to her neck. As their hands touched, she smiled warmly. Gerard looked happier than she had ever seen him as he held his wife tightly then looked to Lucy.

"Fight the fight, no matter what's lost. No matter the sacrifice," he said to her.

With that, Azrael opened his cloak and said, "It's time." He shrouded the trio, and in an instant, they were gone. Lucy heard Jaso calling for his father.

"Dad! Please don't go! I need you; stay with me," Jaso pleaded.

Tears falling from her eyes, "He's gone," Lucy told them. "I saw him go."

"You saw him leave?" Stan asked. "How?"

Lucy had a blank stare on her face; eyes fixed on her friend laying in the bed. "I saw Azrael come into the room. Gerard's spirit left his body, but it was a younger him. Alyssa and Emily came to show him the way."

"You saw them come to take him? How is that possible?" asked Jaso.

Lucy held up the key of knowledge that was still in her hand. She looked at the sparkling gem and realized, "I'm connected to death now. Gerard spoke to me before he left. He told me to fight the fight ..."

Jaso turned back to his father's body trying to fight back more tears. "No matter what's lost. No matter the sacrifice. He told me that more times than I can count."

"I believe he told us all that at one time or another," said James from the back of the room.

"We will prepare his resting place. He has fought a good fight. His body just couldn't take the pressure from the atomic armor anymore," said Stan. She put her arms around Jaso. "We are here if you need us, son."

"Please, don't call me that." Jaso pulled away from her, "I'm sorry. I have a lot to process right now. Just please don't call me that." He lowered his head and walked from the room.

"His heart is heavy right now; he'll come around," Lucy told her.

Stan smiled, "I hope so, kiddo. I just lost his father, I don't want to lose him as well."

19 The Key Comes Home

That evening in the lounge, all were gathered around with Jaso at the head of the table where Gerard had been for over five decades. You could feel the sadness radiating from every member there. Even Billy, the kid Lucy thought didn't have a heart, was in the corner alone, sobbing.

"This is a time of great sadness, yet we have cause to celebrate. We lost a powerful force from within the Synod of Reaping. A loyal warrior to the cause. My father dedicated his life to the brotherhood because he recognized he had a chance to make a difference. He gave a voice to those who had been stricken silent by the cold grasp of the Countess." Jaso took a second to compose himself. "I had the honor of telling him we had finally found and recovered the first key of Lazarus in his lifetime. He died knowing we had struck a blow to the Countess, and for the first time, and not the last, she felt fear!"

Everyone in the room gave a cheer. Jaso, whether he wanted it or not, just stepped into his father's shoes as leader of the Synod of Reaping.

"We faced the Countess and her army, and I am proud to say we sent her running back to the shadows," Jaso said while pounding his fist onto the table in front of him. "Everyone in this room is a part of something bigger, something better than we can ever be on our own; we are family. My father would not want us to mourn him, but to celebrate him."

Stan stepped to the front as Jaso stepped down. "We will lay Gerard Hamilton to rest next to his wife and daughter. He gave instructions on where and how to say goodbye. I urge you to fill your minds with what he meant to you, this organization, and to know we will prevail."

Each one stood and said what Gerard had done for them. From the newest to the veterans, not a dry eye was left. To Lucy's surprise, she heard a voice in the back that caught her attention.

"Drr. Hamilton vas life-line to me as I kame to zis kountrry. He saved me. I needed help when voices inside dis head shouted too loud. To be RReaper vas a rresponsibility and honorr. He showed me ver my place vas. I vill miss him grreatly. хорошо путешествуй, мой друг."

After the vigil, Lucy found Jemison. "Why didn't you tell me you were a Reaper?"

Jemison smiled and wrung his hat in his hands, "I have my place in da kab. I help zose who help da vorld. I am not varrior, tinkerr, orr medic, but I kan watch out for oders that arre."

Lucy hugged him tight and whispered in his ear, "Thank you, Jemison, you do your job perfectly. You should be proud."

"If you ever need rride, you kall Jemison," he said with a huge smile.

Lucy gave a nod, "Yes, sir."

Micah walked up to Lucy. "You okay?"

"I will be," she said. "We all will be. We are a family. And this family always has each other's six."

"Yes, ma'am we do." He put his arm around her shoulder. "I'm thinking because of you; this family can see the end; and the possibility of a new future."

"I hope so, Micah. I don't think my heart could take losing loved ones and it be for nothing."

LATER THAT EVENING, Jaso, Stan, and Lucy joined James in the workshop.

"We need to make sure the key is safe and secure," said Jaso.

James placed a beautiful box onto the table. The design was simple yet complex, rustic and futuristic at the same time.

"This is not as unique as the enigma boxes Conrad made, but I believe it will serve its purpose," James told them.

The box was the size of a book, and had gears of all sizes lining the face. Small piston rods pushed by the gears formed a tooth like grid along the edges. The pistons shone like highly polished mirror.

"I designed the box to only open if two of us are present, and touching the sensors at the same time while entering a pin code with your other hand," James explained.

"What if the box is stolen?" asked Stan. "It's not too big to just grab and run."

James smiled. "The material is immune to all known acids, it can withstand a direct hit from the Delta charge, and it will not rust. This is the hardest material I have ever worked with. It is surprisingly easy to form; I'm trying to figure out a way to make armor out of it!" James's eyes flashed with excitement talking about the metal and the box.

"Where is Micah? Shouldn't he be here too?" asked Lucy.

Jaso told her, "We sent him on a supply run, he should be back by now. We will fill him in on the details later. Now, what do we do with this box?"

"I need to set our fingerprints to the sensors. Each one needs to input the same code that will open the gears. It can be numbers, letters or a combination of both," James told them. "So, what do we want it to be?"

"How about 2058 for the year we got the key?" asked Stan.

Jaso spoke up, "I like GH58 for father."

"Those are good," said James. "What about ..."

"Hope."

Everyone looked to Lucy. She was staring at the box with memories of Gerard and Conrad filling her heart and mind.

"Hope for us all. Without hope, we wouldn't be here," she said.

They looked at each other; smiles started forming all around.

"Hope it is!" exclaimed James. "I like it. Now, we will each place our hands on the corners, and I'll load in the letters."

With a turn, a twist, and some pressing of buttons, each one placed their hand as James set the code. The box opened, and a padded compartment rose to the top with five open slots, one for each key, formed into the red velvet layer. Lucy took the key from around her neck and placed it into the first slot.

"We have taken a huge step forward in the fight against the Countess. My father and all the Reapers before us would be proud," Jaso said in a solemn tone.

"I feel them rejoicing with us," Stan said as she placed her hand over her heart.

"This is for you, Gramps. We will end this," Lucy said as the tears rolled down her face once more.

James reset the locks and the key was secure.

"Where will we keep the box?" asked Stan. "The Countess may not be able to get into the box, but she could steal it. If we can't unite all five keys, it will be at a stalemate."

James smiled so big you could count his molars through the gray and black facial hair. "We have somewhere in mind that the Countess wouldn't dare to go. Hell, I wouldn't go there myself." As he said that, he and Lucy shared a high five.

Stan searched their faces trying to make sense of it all. "Okay, I officially have no clue what you are talking about."

Lucy spoke up. "I'm asking Azrael to watch over it."

"You're doing what now?" asked Stan.

James was absolutely giddy, bouncing up and down in his chair. "It's brilliant, is it not! If she enters his domain, POOF, she will lose her power over the Shadow Gem of Lazarus, and we win anyway."

"As long as he agrees, and cooperates," Lucy said while tilting her head.

Jaso clasped his hands in from of him with a loud clap, "Well, with that, I need a drink. Care to join me, Stan? We need to discuss some things." He smiled back at her. "Family things."

Stan grabbed him and wrapped her arms around him, holding him tight. "It makes me so happy to hear you say that!" she said. "I don't think we want to be here for this part anyway."

They left the workshop leaving James and Lucy with the key holder.

"Do you need me to, um, help with... you know, him?" James asked almost in a whisper.

"Nah, I got this. You can head upstairs with the others. Will you get Flo to fire me up a grilled cheese?" she gave a nod toward the elevator. "Ask her for two; I'm sure Micah will want one when he gets back."

James gave her a nod, "You did good, kid. You are a special young lady, but you don't know the potential that Conrad gave you. If you want, I will help you understand it all, to harness it." He wheeled up beside her and tapped her on the arm. "There is more to you than you know. Now, I'm not your grandfather, but I am a pretty good tinker, if I do say so myself."

She laughed and took his hand, "Thank you, James. I'm sure I'll need help understanding all of this. I'm going to try and take it slow to fully grasp it all."

"Good idea." James kissed her hand and then headed toward the elevator. "We will get her. Finally get her."

The doors closed and Lucy was alone.

20 Enter the Deadman

Lucy walked around the workshop grasping onto the key holder box. She pulled up a seat at the main work table and ran a finger over the gears.

"Well, Gramps. I don't remember everything, but it's only fitting I end up here in this workshop where you gave me a second chance at life. In turn, we are trying to give the world a second chance," she said out loud. Lucy rubbed her elbow, feeling the scar running across her skin. "I don't fully know why you gave me this opportunity, but... thank you."

As Lucy looked around the workshop, she saw flashes of past images of her grandfather working alongside James, alive and passionate about his work. She saw the two of them building glorious devices, deadly tinkers, and wondrous works of engineering. At one point, the image of Conrad seemed to look her way, as if he was real and could see her. He gave a slight nod of his head and a reassuring wink before returning to his work. Lucy wiped the tear rolling down her cheek and took a deep breath. The images faded, and she was alone

She held the box tightly in her arms. Closing her eyes, she filled her mind with thoughts of Azrael. She summoned him to the workshop hoping he wouldn't be angry. The air became still and a puff of frosty breath rolled from Lucy's lips as she whispered his name.

"Azrael."

"Do not think yourself worthy of a position that you can summon the Lord of Death," Azrael said as he loomed over her.

"Well, you're here aren't you? I must be worthy on some level. I need a favor from you," she said.

Azrael boomed, "I do not grant favors, I am the..."

"Yeah, yeah, blah, blah, you're the Lord of Death, I know. Calm down. This will benefit the both of us," she said. "I need you to hold onto this box for me. It holds the Key of Knowledge and will be the placement for all the keys as we collect them. We need to keep them safe until we have all five. Then we can stop Ruina Baxter and you can claim your prize. You do wish to claim the Shadow Gem of Lazarus and take the soul of the one that holds it, don't you?" Lucy held the box out in front of the angel.

She knew she had him. She was offering the chance to take back what was his.

"You are extremely brave, young one," he said. He removed his hood, and peered directly into her eyes. "The deal is struck. Either way, I will claim you. I will grant you easement knowing when you deliver Lazarus to me, you deliver yourself as well," he told her as he took the box. "Keep your faith, Lucy Ducit. Until next time." The angel faded into the shadows of the workshop leaving Lucy alone once again.

"Well, that was reassuring," she said exhaling the burst of breath she had been holding. She ran her fingers through her hair, "I think I need that sandwich now." She walked to the elevator and went to wait for Micah in the mess hall.

MICAH WAS ON HIS WAY back, carrying two large duffel bags down an alleyway leading to the Met. He suddenly stopped, dropping he bags pulling the Sentai blades from his back, and stepped into his battle stance. Realizing who was near he relaxed and sat down on an old wooden crate. Micah placed the swords back into the sheath, and pulled an apple from one of the bags.

"I didn't hurt you, did I?" he asked out loud. "I was worried it was too much."

A shadowy figure emerged from the back of the alley.

"No. I have had worse. You played your part to perfection, my son..."

Micah smiled as a lady's hand covered by a black lace glove touched his cheek. He smiled then took a bite from the apple and watched as the remaining part of the fruit began to wither.

The End

Did you love *The Key of Knowledge*? Then you should read *The Bad Seed* by Michael Lackey!

It was early morning when Zachery Morely's mother asked him to fetch some herbs from the garden. Unknowingly, this simple chore was going to turn into a life-altering event for him and, ultimately, his world. It was during this simple task that he found himself face to face to a powerful unknown being bent on destruction. It was this being... a demon who planted the bad seed, which would give rise to a horrific army. Zachery and his father, George, set off to seek the help of King Gabriel and his court to determine what kind of horrors could come from what looked to be an ordinary tree. It is not until it consumes a living creature and ultimately a human, did they realize this tree housed a demon. Their world was in trouble, and Zachery joins forces with the king and his guards on an epic journey through the lands of men, dwarves, and elves, in search of a hero. Zachery meets wizards and befriends a dragon in this fight against evil, and for all that is good. It is during these epic battles he discovers something- himself. Zachery realizes to find a hero; he had to be one. Through this, he sees that he is more powerful than he ever could imagine. This story will take you on a fast-paced adventure with battles that could determine the future of the world and forges a boy into a hero...

About the Author

Michael Lackey is the author of the Battle for the Heaves and Keys of Lazarus series of young adult novels. He is also an accomplished children's author with the Oswald the Onion series. Follow him on Twitter and Instagram for first announcements and giveaways.

About the Publisher

A Murder of Crows
    One crow for malice,
    Two for mirth,
    Three for a funeral,
    Four for birth,
    Five for silver,
    Six for gold,
    Seven for a story, that should never be told.
    Eight for heaven,
    Nine for a hell.
    Ten to the devil,
    where ever he may dwell.